Love ON THE CAPE

USA TODAY BESTSELLING AUTHOR
MK MEREDITH

This book is a work of fiction. Names, characters, places, and incidents are the product of the author's imagination or are used fictitiously. Any resemblance to actual events, locales, or persons, living or dead, is coincidental.

MK Meredith
P.O. Box 1724
Ashburn, VA 20146
Visit my website at www.mkmeredith.com.

Edited by KR Nadelson and Jessica Snyder
Cover design by Kari March Designs

ISBN: 978-1-7328980-1-1
Manufactured in the United States of America
First Edition June 2017

PRAISE FOR LOVE ON THE CAPE

"*Love on the Cape* is the kind of romance I love best—sexy, deeply emotional, rooted in characters who have had real lives and real traumas, and find love and healing in each other's arms, all beautifully crafted by a writer with brilliant instincts. Don't miss this one."
~ Barbara O'Neal, seven-time RITA Award Winning Author of *How to Bake a Perfect Life*.

"I can't recommend *Love on the Cape* highly enough! This heart-tugging romance struck all the right notes and left me with warm, fuzzy feels! The mega-talented MK Meredith is now on my official 1-click author list and I hope to see her feature more books set on this gorgeous cape!"
~ EpicRomanceReviews

"A must read! I devoured this book. MK Meredith outdid herself again!"
~ BookSnuggle

INTRODUCTION

Hello!

I am so thrilled to share my happy ever afters with you, and I hope you love this book! If you haven't yet, enjoy your introduction to the wonderful town of Cape Van Buren with *One Jingle or Two* **FREE** on all e-retailers. Once you fall in love with Alora and Nate (they're irresistible, LOL!), you won't want to leave.

Which makes me so excited to offer you the opportunity to meet Blayne and Jamie! Just sign up to my mailing list, and I'll send *Honor on the Cape* to your email for download to your favorite reading device!

BTW . . . all of my series are inter-connected.

Hugs, loves, & peanut butter!
MK

To Jessica Snyder.
Your friendship and generous nature
are such beautiful gifts.
Thank you for really seeing me
and loving me anyway.

CHAPTER 1

*L*arkin Sinclair slid her hand down the inside of the well to the second row of bricks until the small handprint settled home under her fingertips. She promised for the thousandth time that she'd start living again. Soon. Though it seemed like an impossibility when a part of her was gone forever.

She skimmed the outline to the pinky finger that faded the closer she got to the end, then to the palm where it was deepest by the thumb. Today, she needed to feel the familiar indentation of her son's palm. She focused on the memory of his small hand with the tight and often sticky grip of his fingers wrapped around one of her own.

The sensation lingered, so she closed her hand to keep it from slipping away. He was with her at the Cape, a peninsula of richly-wooded earth wrapped in a great rocky shore along the coast of Maine. The Atlantic to the east and the town of Cape Van Buren to the west. It called to both her heart and her vocation. The property was a conservationist's dream, and she'd been taking notes since the first day she stepped on the enriched soil.

If not for her work with Conservation Law Foundation, the idea of getting out of bed each morning was daunting at best, impossible at worst. But she'd loved the job since her first day over a decade ago. She'd worked her way up through hard work, a lot of heart, and a passion for the environment.

He would have been seven today, her sweet boy, Archer. If the universe was less cruel and reality not quite so brutal.

But at the Cape, it was as if he embraced her with the rich, isolated earth, and spoke on the gentle July breeze that sighed through the tops of the trees. When she concentrated very hard, his laughter played out on the wind chimes hanging throughout the woods.

The tinkling, playful melody reached her ears, and the corners of her lips pulled up as if they had a mind of their own. There was a measure of relief in the action, a reminder that she hadn't forgotten how. She gripped the locket hanging just above her heart and rubbed the square shape between her thumb and forefinger. One side held a photo of her and Archer from the day he was born; the other side held a photo of the two of them her dear friend Maxine had taken in front of the well the last time she'd seen him. She released her breath on a long, slow sigh.

"Can I help you?"

The deep, masculine voice shot prickles of adrenaline to the surface of her skin, and she jerked so hard the chain around her neck snapped, sending her necklace flying.

"No!" She cried out, lunging toward the opening of the well and grabbing at the air.

Two strong arms wrapped around her waist, halting her forward momentum. "Hold on now...I've got you."

"No. Let me go." She shoved at his hands in a panic then leaned over the well with tears stinging her eyes. A small glint of light reflected from the side a few feet below the rim and relief swept through her in a fierce rush. Her locket had landed precariously close to the edge of a narrow, ragged stone, the broken chain swinging back and forth over the side.

No, no, no. This can't be happening.

She stretched her arm as far as physics and anatomy allowed but she couldn't reach the necklace. Staring at it in abject horror, she prayed it wouldn't drop. "Please don't fall, please don't fall." She blew out a breath against the burning in her chest and tried again.

"Lady, you're going to hurt yourself."

Larkin jerked her head up.

The words were spoken in low, measured beats by a tall man with dark wavy hair and a few day's growth on his jaw that left him looking like a lumberjack, though the half-buttoned dress shirt and low-slung slacks tried to suggest otherwise.

"I don't care. It's my locket." She leaned over the edge, working as hard to reach the necklace as she was at maintaining some measure of composure. "I have to get it."

"Okay, okay. Christ. The last thing I need is some crazy lady falling into the well."

He pulled her from the rim. She didn't care what the guy thought as long as she got her locket back. He stepped to her side, filling the space next to her, and she shifted away just a bit so she could breathe.

Glancing over the edge, he shook his head. "It's too far."

"Then I'll just have to get it myself."

"Lady—" He grabbed her shoulder.

With a jerk, she pulled away. "I didn't ask for your help."

If the guy wasn't going to help, then he needed to get the hell out of her way. Where in the world was Maxine? She glanced at the house then back to the well.

"Okay, okay. Just wait a second."

She pressed against the warm skin where the necklace had hung. He might not understand, but she couldn't lose it. "I have to get it." She looked for a long branch with a flat end. Anything that might hold the locket so she could pull it up.

"Was it your mother's or something?"

"It was from my son and it can't be replaced." The words dragged against her vocal cords like sandpaper. Archer had given her the necklace on the last Mother's Day they'd spent together.

The large man blew out a heavy breath. The kind of sigh that vocalized an unwilling acceptance, and she glanced at him, hoping the sound meant what she thought it might.

"Fine. Let me have a look."

Relief rushed through her and she stepped aside. Grumbling under his breath, he cleared the few buttons on his shirt then shrugged it off his broad shoulders. She coughed into her hand with wide, watering eyes. Nothing on her to-do list from that morning mentioned anything about a bare, well-muscled chest. And the sight of him made her question why not.

He patted her on the back. At least she imagined that was his intent, but each thump almost sent her flying face-first into the ground. She spread her feet wide to gain more balance and, waving him off, swallowed a few times to get her breathing under control again.

"I'm fine. I'm fine. What are you doing?"

He glanced down at the shirt then shoved it into her outstretched hand. "This is a five-hundred-dollar Armani. I'm not about to destroy it on a pile of old stones."

The fabric was warm and the scent of his cologne wafted up around her head as he turned toward the well. He walked the perimeter and tested the integrity of each stone with a nudge. "I might be able to get it. But promise me you're not going to go all kamikaze if I can't."

She held her breath and nodded, though he was the crazy one if he thought for a second she was leaving without it.

Spreading his legs wide, he braced his hip against the edge and leaned over. With one hand holding the top row of stones, he stretched his other toward the necklace, muscles striating down his back with the effort and disappearing below his waistband.

"Hold on to me." He barked the order and she moved without thinking.

But as she reached for him, her mind went blank on where exactly she should anchor him down. She grabbed his hips, but his slacks were slick, so she grabbed his waist, but the heat of his skin shot through her in a shockwave and she let go.

"Hold on! Goddamnit."

"Sorry." She gave herself a shake then wrapped her arms low around his waist and used her body weight to balance him. His surprising heat, his rich, masculine scent. She tried hard to block her senses.

"Shit." His curse echoed from the well.

"Did you get it?"

"Not yet. The damn stones are cutting into my side." Frustration made his words curt and more than a little accusatory.

Regardless of how scratched up he might get, she needed that necklace.

His grunts, interlaced with a few choice swear words, replaced any further conversation. "Almost...just a little farther...a little farther." He shifted forward,

4

and she dropped her hips lower to counterweight the movement, freaking out a little bit as his feet lifted from the ground.

"I got it," he shouted.

"*Oh God.*" She pulled back on him, desperate to get his feet and her necklace safely on solid ground once again.

He straightened and dangled her locket from his fingers.

Gratitude hit her with a swift punch of relief and she launched at him, almost knocking him back off his feet.

"Thank you. Thank you. I was so scared." With her arms wrapped tightly around his waist, she kissed his cheek and squeezed hard, then kissed his cheek once again. Only this time, the rough scruff of his facial hair registered under her lips, and his crisp and spicy scent filled the senses she'd worked so hard to shut down.

She froze then carefully untangled herself from his embrace.

He stared at her with a bemused expression and slowly reached out one more time to give her the necklace.

If the ground would open up and swallow her whole, she'd be forever grateful, but of course it didn't. She'd never been that lucky. Gingerly, she took the chain from him. "I'm sorry for losing my mind for a second. But it means so much to me."

Now that her panic had dissipated, she wasn't sure where to look. His broad shoulders and massive chest were very bare and very—*whoa*. So she looked everywhere but at him, until she finally pulled herself together enough to settle on the chiseled features of his ruggedly handsome face. Her heart thrummed as she stared into dark eyes hooded by equally dark brows, and she paused. It was a feeling she recalled, but almost like an echo of the past rather than a physical certainty.

"Who are you?" She knew the owner of the property quite well, and this sexy knight-in-wrinkly-armor was most certainly not Maxine Van Buren—her surrogate grandmother and one of Archer's favorite people. Truth be told, she was probably a favorite throughout the whole town of Cape Van Buren from North Cove to South Cove, from the Town Square to the tip of the Cape. Maxine got around.

Larkin handed him his shirt but immediately jerked it back. Along the outer edges of his ribs on one side was a line of nasty gashes. "Oh, no." She slung the shirt over her shoulder then reached for him, gently pressing around the perimeter of the wound and hating that she was the cause of it.

He winced, and she met his gaze.

"I'm so sorry. Is Maxine here? She has a first aid kit in the main floor restroom. Janice is always cutting herself with her sheers, or poking herself on the rose bush thorns." She draped his shirt neatly over one arm then grabbed his hand, silently chastising herself for babbling. Janice was Maxine's best friend and a master gardener, but Larkin had no idea if this guy even knew who Maxine was, much less anyone else.

He resisted. "You know my grandmother?"

She made the mistake of glancing back at him only to see that the look on his face had softened in a way that left her fidgety. She gave a mental shake like she used to do with the eight ball anytime the answer displayed didn't make sense. What in the hell was wrong with her? Too many restless nights and not enough human interaction, apparently.

Conversations with Maxine rushed through her brain. She'd known of a grandson, the CEO of Van Buren Enterprises, a big-time developer in New York City. Her friend had spoken fondly of him, but always with a touch of melancholy. She'd say she missed the sweet little boy who'd followed her around like a shadow.

This man standing before her was anything but a little boy. A whistle wanted to accompany the thought, but she flashed a polite smile instead.

Ryker, if she remembered correctly, Ryker Van Buren. He'd left right after high school, never having stepped foot on the estate again—or in town for that matter. Well, until today, so it seemed.

"You must be Maxine's grandson. I'm Larkin Sinclair, a friend of your grandmother's." She pulled on his hand again. "Come on. I want to help get you cleaned up. It's the least I can do."

Recognition swept over his face, further easing the hard lines around his eyes and mouth, but he still resisted. "Ryker," he said in way of introduction. Then he raised a brow. "Larkin, what kind of name is that?"

"What kind of name is Ryker?"

"Touché." He nodded. "Larkin Sinclair. I remember...you had a little boy. Archer. Grandmother talks about you all the time."

This time it wasn't the deep timbre of his voice but the sorrow it held and the use of the past tense that stopped her. She'd *had* a little boy? No. She would always have a little boy—in her heart, her memories. His existence had changed hers the moment he'd been laid upon her chest. He was an extension of herself, an addition that made her better in every way. Now it was as if she'd lost a limb and suffered from phantom pain because she still felt him in her heart, but the knowledge that he was no longer physically here left her with a constant ache.

She turned back with a slight dip of her chin. "Yes, my son's name is Archer."

If he wasn't going to go with her to Maxine's house, she'd at least do what she could with the first aid kit in her glove box. She pinned him with a look. "Stay right there."

Within a few seconds, she returned, carrying bacterial ointment, gauze, and tape. "You don't seem to want to go up to the house. But at least let me take care of the worst of this until you're able to see the doctor."

He laughed, but it was more of a "yeah right" than anything else, and it left her a bit off-kilter as the deep, rough sound skittered along her spine. He lifted his hand toward her then stopped and slid it into his front pocket as she gently absorbed as much of the blood as she could with the gauze, doing her best not to touch his bare skin again. He leaned away, but she ignored him and finished her task.

"You really don't need to do this," he said gruffly.

"Are you always so stubborn when someone wants to help you?"

This time, he ignored her. "Archer...he loved puzzles. Made a few for Grandmother if I remember correctly."

She paused as an image of her son teaching Maxine and the North Cove Mavens how to assemble one of his latest creations brought a fresh wave of tears to her eyes. She blinked through them while loading three large, fresh squares of gauze with ointment. "Yes, Maxine would go on and on about how he was the puzzle master. We even have a cat named Puzzle."

She smiled at him. "He loved your grandmother very much." Sweeping her hand out to the grounds around them, she added, "He loved the Cape. We came to visit every month."

Their visits often overlapped with the North Cove Mavens' monthly meetings-four ladies who lived north of the Cape and sparred good-naturedly over superiority with the South Cove Madams. Something about two sisters who had lived on opposite sides of the town and the one boy who had captured both their hearts. The feud's history was as old as the town itself.

Ryker reached out his hand, and this time left it there.

She stared at it, the urge to take it leaving her more than a little confused.

"It's nice to meet you." He chuckled wryly.

Slipping her hand into his much larger and warmer one, she couldn't pull her eyes away from how completely it engulfed hers. He was the first man she'd touched in two years. His palm was rough and solid, and she wanted to hold it longer, to press her palm more tightly against it. But instead, she opened her fingers and slid from his grip, hoping he didn't notice the slight tremble in her fingers as she turned to press the bandage carefully in place.

"Am I making you nervous?" he asked with a questioning look.

"You saved my locket." Her words didn't make any more sense to her than they would to him. Something about the man left her wanting in a way she'd been afraid she'd forgotten.

His bark of laughter echoed off the trees, and if the look on his face was any indication, the action surprised him as much as it had her. "You don't have much of a poker face, do you?"

"I've never been one to play games."

He grinned—if you could call it that—in approval. It was as if his lips couldn't remember how, so only one side was successful. "Only puzzles?"

She sighed, letting the building tension slide down her back. "Definitely puzzles." She finished taping him up. Giving his muscular shoulder an awkward pat, she stepped back.

Ryker pushed to his feet then ran his thick fingers along the rim of the well, and she couldn't look away. "You're welcome here whenever you want. At least until I sell it. Since Grandmother moved out—"

Larkin snapped her head up, and a low buzzing drowned out the rest of his words. *Sell it?* What was he talking about? "Maxine moved out? Where? Why?"

He stepped in front of her again and pinned her with his gaze. "She didn't tell you?"

Moving back just a bit, needing a little room to breathe, she furrowed her brow. "No. I was here last month, but she never said a word." She thought hard about their last visit. "Maxine had mentioned wanting to be in town because she liked the idea of walking everywhere, but I had no idea she was serious."

"She wants to downsize and live it up while she's still young, and Van Buren Square is where all the action is, apparently." He chuckled with an indulgent shake of his head. "Her words."

"So, *you* are the new owner? I thought you didn't even like it here."

"I grew up here." His eyes shuttered and he turned back toward the house. "This is my home." His voice caught on "home" and something passed over his hard features, almost as if the word had a bad taste to it.

She wanted to push for more but the tense set of his shoulders stopped her.

What was she going to do? She'd visited the well and puttered about the property as often as she'd wanted over the past two years. Anytime she needed to feel close to her son. No pressure, no problem.

But not anymore. And maybe never again. Her chest tightened painfully and she locked her eyes on the well. He couldn't sell the Cape.

Blinking back tears, she stepped away. "Okay, then. Nice to meet you, and thanks for saving my locket." Pulling in a breath of salty ocean air against the tightness in her chest, she looked past the well to the expanse of rich green grass and colorful gardens, then farther still to the lighthouse that stood tall and sure at the water's edge.

She walked toward her car parked a ways down the gravel driveway, resisting the urge to run.

"No problem. I'll see you soon."

She paused. "Why?"

This time he didn't chuckle but merely raised a brow. "Why? You sure know how to make a man feel wanted, Ms. Sinclair."

Her brain struggled to keep up against her rising panic but insulting the owner was no way to ensure her entry to the Cape or to try to get him to change his mind. "I'm so sorry. I just meant—"

"I'll see you again because, like I said, you're welcome here as long as the Cape is still mine. I'm glad you didn't lose your locket."

Her world was crashing down around her, and he was smiling and waving goodbye like they were new friends. She opened her car door, forcing words from her mouth. "Thank you."

He was selling the Cape.

He may have saved her locket but her connection to Archer might be lost forever.

∽

*L*arkin pushed through the doors of the Flat Iron Coffeehouse, a swanky coffee shop on the south side of Cape Van Buren. A cross between urban chic and preppy tech, it greeted her with the welcoming aroma of beans and brew while the overhead music encouraged her to sit down and settle in. Though *settled* was the last thing she felt.

Every nerve ending was exposed and raw with worry.

She needed answers to prove the last few hours were nothing more than a horrible misunderstanding. A quick call to her dad had helped center her a bit, as it always did. Her dad had been her rock and greatest fan since she'd taken her first breath, and the feeling was mutual.

She was close to both her parents. They were always there for her but never intrusive. Though she believed the reason they gave her so much space was because all they had to do was ask around town to check in. Growing up in Cape Van Buren her whole life meant there were no secrets. It was often annoying but mostly a comfort.

Though nothing was comfortable now. And it wouldn't be until she had some answers.

She scanned the room for Maxine, finding her waving from a cozy table toward the back of the shop. She was a silver fox with her straight, chic hair slightly longer in the front than the back, dressed in a sophisticated sleeveless jumpsuit of vibrant purple. No black for her friend. Maxine always said there was no reason to wear it if she wasn't dead. Larkin admired the woman's zest for life.

Especially since she didn't feel much of anything these days.

Ryker's crooked attempt at a grin popped into her mind but she ruthlessly shoved it away. Her interaction with him had sparked the most sensations she'd experienced in a long time, but much of that was surely due to the fact he might take away her only reason for waking up each morning.

Maxine studied her as she approached then pushed up from the table with a worried look on her face. Pulling her in, she wrapped her in a tight embrace.

"Larkin, what's wrong?"

The sensation of being held was scarce these days, so Larkin embraced her tight, eking out the comfort. "Please tell me the sale isn't final."

Maxine sighed then gestured for Larkin to join her at the table. The older woman sipped from her cup as their server set a café au lait between them. "I ordered for you."

"Thank you." Larkin sat down then wrapped her chilled fingers around the warm porcelain, sporting a silver stripe around the rim.

Maxine spoke softly. "It's final, my dear."

Larkin sputtered, "But...what about the well? About how special the land is? Not just to me, but the environment? The plants and animals there will be destroyed."

How many times had she encouraged her friend to have the land studied for conservation? It was a very special piece of property that provided a unique habitat for a handful of threatened species of plants and animals. She'd spotted it upon her very first visit. As a wildlife conservation expert, she had a trained eye and a passion for preservation. And Cape Van Buren was as good as it got.

"If I'm turning the Cape over to anyone, it's family. You must understand. Your parents would move heaven and hell for you, as you would have for Archer." She pressed her lips together. "In any case, Ryker would never kick you off the property, no matter what he might have told you." She sent a questioning look that spoke of all the trouble he'd be in if he had. "He didn't, did he?"

The fact that she asked increased Larkin's worry. "No, no. He was actually quite pleasant and even saved my locket from ending up at the bottom of the well."

"No one has ever accused my grandson of being pleasant. Brooding maybe, or detached, but never pleasant."

Larkin looked at her friend and swallowed hard. "He said he's selling it."

Maxine stiffened. "He was probably just being ornery, but either way, the Cape belongs to him now." The corners of her mouth rose a fraction in a forced half-smile. "Whatever he decides, I'm sure he'll do right by it."

"I wish I had your confidence." Larkin traced the geometric shape along the border of her place mat with her finger. "Why didn't you tell me you were selling? I would have made an offer."

Maxine's fingers fluttered on the table as if she didn't know what to do with them until they found their way around her cup once again. "He's my grandson, my dear." She ditched the cup and reached across the table, grabbing Larkin's hands. "And you are like a granddaughter to me. You've been a loyal, loving, and beautiful friend. But Ryker had a difficult childhood that chased him from his home. I needed to give him a chance to find his way back."

"You've said he had it rough, but—"

"I wish it had simply been rough. And I'm afraid I'd failed him. But now I have a chance to make up for it. I have to do something." She leaned back. "I hope he won't take the Cape from you, but I couldn't keep it from him."

"How could you have failed him? All you've ever said is how you wished you could spend more time together, how you wished he'd come home more often. Instead, you went to him every time."

"I did. The memories were too much for him here, but me putting the Cape up for sale has done what my cajoling never could." She emptied her cup then smiled. "It brought him home."

There was no mistaking the love in her friend's eyes or the flicker of hope. Hope that Larkin didn't share.

"Which reminds me, if you happen to see him before I do, tell him I'll be by to go through the attic. The Cape may be his, but no one's messing with my moonshine."

"I will." The legends of Maxine's moonshine and the trouble she'd gotten into time and again were well known around these parts. But Larkin didn't blame her. The stuff went down easy and hit like a cannon. People would line up cash in hand—which was the problem. Making it wasn't necessarily illegal but selling it was.

The change in subject ended any chance that it was all a terrible misunderstanding, leaving her with only one other option.

If Ryker was bent on selling the Cape then she'd have to be the first to put in an offer.

CHAPTER 2

"What don't you understand about the word 'more?'" Ryker grated out, tired from a restless night of haunting dreams starring a green-eyed beauty hanging precariously from the stones of a bottomless well. No matter how hard he tried, he couldn't reach her, and the echoes of his father's mocking laughter still rung in his ears.

Ryker was the kind of boss that often worked alongside his men, and he was itching to feel the burn of hard physical labor. The apparent lack of understanding and delays in breaking ground was more than frustrating—it was unacceptable.

"But, sir, we understood that Mr. Brennan explained to you the dangers of—"

Ryker struck fast. "Mr. Brennan isn't cutting your paycheck, now is he?" His attorney and best friend, Mitch Brennan, had indeed gone over the risks. But they were Ryker's to take.

His men fell silent, then all four heads turned as someone rounded the massive fountain in the center of the drive.

Who the hell was here now? If this kept up, he'd have to lock the gate at the main entrance. Since it opened right up to the town of Cape Van Buren, everyone took it as a damned invitation.

It was a helluva lot different from his life in New York where no one even made it to his front door without an invitation.

Stepping past the round, plaid-covered belly of Charlie Jones, his lead contractor, Ryker froze and swore under his breath. Larkin's halo of blond hair reflected the sun, stray wisps floating about in the early morning sea breeze.

He absently rubbed his side as she crossed the driveway and marched toward the well with purpose, her long, flowing skirt whipping about her long, sexy legs. She carried her willowy frame with such confidence the men's discussion fell by the wayside. Charlie's ginger bearded chin dropped to his chest, and Ryker would have found it funny if he hadn't been staring right along with him.

Clearing his throat, he handed over the large map. "Excuse me a moment, gentlemen."

He walked slowly toward the well, drinking her in with interest. A sense of déjà vu washed over him as she bent over the well, but this time she dropped a penny. Her lips moved in a whisper that he couldn't quite catch. Something about wishes. Too bad wishes rarely came true.

"Please don't drop your necklace again," he called out.

With her hand over her brow to shield out the sun, she squinted at him with a smile. A small dimple appeared just below the left corner of her mouth and he had to force himself to meet her eyes instead of studying it further. Damn it. Brilliant green eyes, reflecting her emotions like the sun on waves, nearly knocked the wind out of him, and he had to shake it off.

"Making a wish?"

"As often as I can." She ran her fingers along the uneven rim of the well and looked out across the lawn. "Archer always hung half his little body over the side like you did yesterday in order to watch his penny splash and disappear to the very bottom. He'd say only then could wishes be made. Scared the crap out of me more than once." She met his gaze with a bittersweet sigh.

"I can imagine." Though he'd never have children of his own. His past was something he was determined to keep locked away where it belonged—the fear and sadness born from those dark years along with it. Having a family, letting someone in that close, would surely open the gates. His childhood was an ugly legacy that would end with him. But he could still understand her fear.

She studied him, chewing her bottom lip.

His eyes kept dipping to her mouth in search of the damn dimple, and it took more effort than it should have to maintain eye contact.

"So, how are you?" she asked.

He sighed at the question, trying to be patient, but he paid the men waiting for him by the hour, and she was more of a distraction than they needed today. He couldn't imagine she came out all this way for small talk.

"Very busy." He indicated the men a few yards behind him.

"Of course." She laughed in a soft tone, the kind meant to hide embarrassment but which often simply magnified it.

"Why are you here?" *On the Cape and in my dreams?* The question popped into his head before he could shut it out, and he rubbed the back of his neck.

"Maxine wanted me to tell you she'd be by to go through the attic. You have to help her."

"And you came all the way out here to tell me that?" There was no doubt in his mind that his grandmother sent her so he couldn't say no. Maxine could manipulate the skin off a snake and onto her shoes if she wanted to—she was that good.

Larkin stared into his eyes, and for a brief second he wished he had a penny to throw in the well for insight into her thoughts.

"I had a bit of a rough day yesterday. A visit to the Cape kind of makes it all better."

He snorted. "Yeah...not for me."

She stepped toward him. "How can you say that? It's—"

With a narrowed look, he raised a hand to stop her, steeling himself against the emotion in her voice. "You and Maxine were good friends. Don't tell me she never told you how bad things used to be here."

Larkin pressed her lips together as a blush rushed across her chest at the reference to his father's abuse. "No, she did. I'm sorry. It's just very hard to reconcile the hard life of the little boy who lived here with..." She waved her hand at him. "I forgot."

He winced, crossing his arms over his chest. "I wish I could."

"I'm sorry. I wasn't thinking." She grabbed his forearm gently.

The soft slide of her hand demanded his attention, reminding him of yesterday when they'd been on his skin, tending to his scrapes, and he glanced down at his arm. Dark, heated thoughts furrowed his brows. She was a gorgeous woman, there was no arguing that, but she was a complication.

One who knew too much pain and not enough pleasure, and it was something he could see no matter how high she lifted her chin or how straight she

15

held her back. A constant reminder that she was not a woman to be toyed with. She'd already had a ton of shit handed her way; she certainly didn't need any of his own personal brand. His pockets were full of it.

An uncomfortable awareness crept into her eyes, and she slowly dropped her hand to her side. He wished she hadn't—which didn't sit well with him at all.

With a step back, he motioned to her face. "What's going on here?"

Confused, she studied the front of her shirt. "I don't know what you mean. I—"

"It's like an immediate sunburn."

Mortification joined the blush that now reached her hairline. Sucking in a breath, she waved her hand like a fan and rubbed the spot he'd almost touched with her other. "Never mind. I'm just warm."

He glanced at the sweater she had tied at her waist. "Then why are you wearing a sweater? It's summer."

Ignoring him, she pointed over his shoulder. "What are you doing with those men?"

Ryker studied her a beat. She hadn't been happy with the news of him selling the Cape, but better she accept it now. "Those men are land surveyors."

"What are they doing? Are you planning an addition? Because I have a serious offer I'd like you to consider." Tension radiated from her, tightening his own muscles, and he forced himself to relax.

"Of sorts." He could barely imagine what she had in mind. With the husky timbre of her voice, when she said the word *offer*, it sounded more like an indecent proposal. One he'd like to take her up on but knew he couldn't. With a wink he hoped would ease the heaviness around them, he asked, "An offer? What do you have in mind?"

"Oh…" She released a nervous laugh. "Will you go for a walk with me?" She shifted from one foot to the other. "I know you're busy, but this is important."

He shook his head. "Ms. Sinclair—"

"Larkin," she corrected.

Against all logic, he loved the way her name felt as it rolled off his tongue. "Larkin. I really must get back."

With steely determination, she pinned him with her gaze and pulled in a breath. "Since you're selling the Cape, I'd like to make an offer."

He couldn't have been more shocked if she'd suggested paying him one hundred thousand dollars to sleep with her—*Indecent Proposal*-style. He cleared his throat. Twice.

"Miss Sinclair."

"Larkin."

He dipped his chin. "Larkin. You can't possibly—"

He followed her gaze back to the Victorian with its navy-and-gold trim. It was almost a gothic look with the eggplant siding, but somehow softer, and perfectly suited to the moody, rocky shores and wooded lands of the Cape. It would make an ideal community building.

He stepped between her and the house until she met his gaze. Low and gentle, he said, "I'm developing the property, Larkin. You couldn't possibly match that kind of profit."

Her mouth dropped open, then closed, and opened again as she processed his words. "Developing the Cape? You mean with houses?"

"Exactly." He hated the look of panic on her lovely features, but she needed to understand the finality of his plans. "This place has brought me nothing but pain. It's about time it gives me something positive, something to make up for the hell of living here all those years. It's been in the works since last fall."

The one thing his past had given him was a very pragmatic look on life, a keen ability to act on cold hard logic, and an immunity toward emotion. Usually.

"But, Ryker." She cleared her throat. "Mr. Van Buren, surely you can see it wasn't the Cape but the circumstances. Please don't do this."

"When I step onto this property, do you know the first thing I remember? My father's fist slamming into my face...more than once."

She sucked in her breath.

It might sound harsh but it was the only way for her to understand how serious he was. Sugarcoating had never been one of his strengths.

"I'm so sorry." She pressed a hand to her stomach. She reached out to him, but he pulled away abruptly. The pain in her eyes cut deep, but the pity there raised his walls like nothing else could. He didn't need anyone's pity and he sure as hell didn't want it.

She squeezed her hands into fists at her sides.

"I understand you're upset. But selling the Cape to you isn't an option." He cracked his neck, the *snap-snap* reverberating loud in the silence between them. "Surely you didn't think you could keep up these visits indefinitely?"

It took two tries, but she said, "I'm not upset about the Cape, I'm upset for the little boy who grew up here." She pressed her lips together, stilling their quiver. "And to answer your very insensitive question: Yes, I absolutely thought I'd always be able to visit. Maxine's like family. I live just off the water of the North Cove and can see the lighthouse from my kitchen window. I never imagined she'd sell it."

Tears welled in her eyes, making the green sparkle as if cut by a master artisan, but he ignored her silent plea. He'd spent his childhood putting everyone before himself in order to keep them safe from his father. He'd believed every threat his dad had made. The man was filled with so much ugly; he didn't see people, only punching bags. Ryker had to do this for himself now. It was the only way he might be able to close up the gaping hole inside of him and finally move forward.

He pulled in a rough breath. "Well, she did. To me. And now I'm going to put it to good use. Besides, there's more to this whole venture. My company is invested already. It's not just personal but also business."

Larkin peeked at the well then blinked back the tears threatening to spill and pulled her shoulders back.

"Please. There must be another way. You must see—"

"Are you about ready, Mr. Van Buren?" One of the surveyors yelled to Ryker. He held up the now-rolled map and shook it back and forth.

On a sigh, Ryker lightly took her hands, which were clenched in a white-knuckled grip at her waist. "I'm sorry, but this is happening."

She stared at the ground. "But you don't understand."

"You're going to be okay, Larkin Sinclair." He squeezed her hands one more time in reassurance, though his words sounded more like a command. He had to make sure she heard him.

He released her and walked back toward his men. They rolled out the map on the large work table and bent over it once again. He listened to their words at first, but couldn't focus with Larkin standing where he'd left her as if she'd forgotten how to put one foot in front of the other.

He moved toward her to quietly demand she come back another time but slowed as she circled the well. She slipped one hand over the edge and held it there then dropped a penny with her other.

What in the hell was the woman doing now?

She waited a moment, then her whisper echoed from the bottom of the well, just barely reaching his ears. "Don't worry, Archer, I waited for the penny to land on the bottom before making my wish." Then she turned away, heading toward one of the trails that weaved through the wooded acreage.

"Van Buren, can we get this show on the road?"

Ignoring the request, he followed the same path Larkin had taken around the well and peered over the edge.

His heart squeezed painfully. There along the second row of bricks were the handprints of a child.

～

*L*arkin took shallow breaths against the rising tide of panic-stricken tears threatening her calm façade. She feared that once she started crying, she might not be able to stop. And the last thing she wanted was for Ryker to be a witness to one of her breaks.

Hurrying to put distance between herself and the chattering conversation about destroying her beloved Cape, she traced the familiar path she'd taken many times before into the shadowed entrance of the woods. It was like stepping through a portal into a whole new dimension. Instead of a world brightened by the warmth of the sun and the diamond waves crashing along the rocky shores, it softened into an emerald velvet, redolent with the scent of lush earth, and blessed by a muffled quality only possible through the embrace of mother nature.

She pulled in a deep breath, letting it out on a shuddering sigh.

"Larkin, wait."

Ryker's husky voice sounded behind her, and she blinked rapidly to erase any signs of distress before she turned around. "Look, I know you're busy. I'll leave in just a bit."

"No, I—" He raked his hand through his hair as if he didn't know what to do with it otherwise.

Well, she didn't have it in her to worry too much about his discomfort with her still being on his property. She needed some peace, so she was going to take it. Who knew how much longer she could before the jeweled woods were cut down to make room for a fabricated mockery of hearth and homes?

"I don't like seeing you upset."

19

She glared. "We've already established my feelings don't matter." She sounded waspish and regretted it immediately, but her heart didn't have any room for niceties at the moment.

"So mine don't matter either?" His soft tone skittered along her skin.

She raised her hand then dropped it. "I'm sorry. That wasn't fair of me." Needing to move, she continued along the trail.

He stepped alongside her and she was instantly enveloped by his warm, masculine scent. It made her think of stormy waters and high winds, both a heat and a lightness to it, forcing her to take a deeper breath to figure it out.

"You know these woods well?" he asked.

She looked at the boulder along the first bend in the trail, wrapped on one side by the weathered gray-brown bark of a large red maple spotted with a vibrant moss—all three entities sharing the same sacred space.

She trailed her fingertips along the spongy green marks that Archer used to call leprechaun droppings. The ache in her heart intensified. "I do. My son and I explored them on every visit." Dropping her hand to her side, she continued. "You?"

He dipped his chin. The muscles along his jaw ticked as he clenched them in some sort of struggle for control. "They gave me shelter more than once."

She felt like there was something more behind his words but he offered nothing else.

A butterfly flitted between them and settled on the low hanging branch of a proud oak. The delicate creature's back was a bright blue that looked like velvet until its wings lifted to reveal a soft white underside speckled with dark dots.

"Huh, that's one I'm not too familiar with, but I've seen it before." He paused to watch it flutter.

Larkin stilled, staring at the butterfly, then a slow smile curved her lips along with an idea. A small fissure of possibility streaked through her heart. "A crowberry blue. One of Archer's favorites. It's very rare, but there's a small, thriving population here on the Cape that doesn't exist anywhere else in the area."

His eyes widened in surprise. "Really?" Focusing his attention more closely on the butterfly, he gave a non-committal grunt of wonder, and she wanted to kick him in the shin. When he developed the property, their habitat would be destroyed to house soccer moms and man caves.

A bit farther down the path, Ryker raised a hand. "Wait. Shhhh." He stopped, holding his finger to his lips. She couldn't tear her gaze away from how the pad of his finger pushed into the generous softness of his mouth. Her mind immediately focused on what it would feel like if her own lips replaced his finger. She pressed her mouth into a thin line against the sensation.

A low buzzing energy finally broke through her distracted haze, and she followed his line of sight to a cloud of honey bees swarming one of several beehive collections scattered around the Cape. There were at least five small apiaries if she remembered correctly.

He glanced at her. "Has Maxine said anything to you about a hired beekeeper for the property?"

She shook her head and took a step back. Where was her cat Puzzle when she needed him? He was a terror to bees and somehow never got stung. Archer had loved to follow him around the yard on his hunts, leaving Larkin to make sure her little boy never got stung. Too bad she couldn't say the same for herself.

Being a coward in front of Ryker was not on her wish list, but if one of those suckers even turned one beady eye her way, she'd beat an Olympic sprinter to the safety of her car.

He pinned her with a raised brow. "Going somewhere?"

She swallowed, pulling her hair over her shoulder and holding on to it like a safety rope. "If you say they won't bother me if I don't bother them, I'll punch you."

A soft chuckle caressed her ears followed by his arm thrown over her shoulder. "You're afraid of bees?"

She scowled in an I'm-not-the-dumb-one kind of way. "At least one of us here has some intelligence." She'd always given herself credit in the past anyway, but the hairs on his arm tickled the sensitive skin along the back of her exposed neck, and the heat of his side warmed her from shoulder to hip in a way that muddled her thinking and made her question her original self-assessment.

"You're blushing again."

With a scowl, she pushed his arm from her shoulders, ignoring the deep bass of his laugh, and swearing under her breath at her damn tattletale curse of a lifetime. How many times had it ruined any poker face she'd mastered? Too many to count. And every time he touched her only added to that humiliating, growing number.

Turning back to retrace their steps toward her car, she swallowed hard, forcing the emotions clawing up her throat back down where they needed to stay.

Ryker fell into step next to her with a quick glance back at the hive. "Swarming the way they are, the bees look honey-bound. I need to give Grandmother a call."

She slowed her pace and looked at him. Curiosity now layered on top of intrigue and something she didn't want to think about yet. "You know about beekeeping?"

Watching his concerned expression morph into a blank veneer was telling. His eyes were now guarded and his jaw set once again.

"My grandfather. I used to help him all the time when I was a kid...until we lost him. I was fifteen, but I remember that day like it was yesterday."

He pretended he was fine but the tension radiating from his body was like a heavy wind buffeting her as she walked.

"What do you mean by honey-bound?"

They stepped up to a small clearing where Maxine had placed a long park bench flanked on both sides by an array of red hummingbird feeders. The swift little birds swarmed about much like the bees, frustrated to find the wells dry. "They need food." She pointed out absently as she sat down.

"I'll put some out after I finish for the day. Anyway, honey-bound is when the hives are over-filled with honey. The bees begin to swarm and productivity will go down. If we're not careful the queen might leave to find more room."

"I'd like to say I'd be disappointed but..." She trailed off. The conservationist in her struggled with her fear. The honey bees were a gift—if only they didn't have to come with stingers. She was tired of feeling pain from something that was so inherently beautiful.

He grinned. "I never pegged you for a scaredy-cat."

"Well, you don't know me very well." She shrugged. As long as the bees stayed on their side, she'd stay on hers. If the universe would let her keep the Cape, she'd even share.

"I need to get back to work. Are you going to be okay?" His question both irritated and touched her.

"Is that why you followed me?" She studied the hard, square line of his jaw and his dark, heavy brow that leaned toward brooding even when he wasn't.

Awareness rushed through her as she imagined what it would be like to be the recipient of that hard stare out of interest instead of pity.

A small spotted salamander skittered across some moss that trailed beneath the bench. "Oh, look," she whispered. Carefully, she twisted and bent forward, placing her hand slowly just in front of the dark blue critter. Its little yellow spots made her think of the high wire acts and funnel cakes of her youth.

The salamander crawled onto her palm, and she straightened, careful not to scare the little guy. "Oh, my gosh," she whispered. Looking over one shoulder then the other, she said, "I bet there's a small vernal pool nearby."

Ryker raised a brow as he checked out the amphibian in her hand.

"A small, temporary pool of water used for breeding," she explained.

He looked at her with a curious expression in his gaze. "You are full of surprises."

"I really am." She nodded her agreement with a playfully haughty air. She was warming to her new idea by the minute. He didn't know the half of it, but he would very soon if she got her way.

On their way back toward her car, she tried one more time. "Even with the beautiful creatures living on this land, you won't reconsider?"

A huge gusting breath was her answer. One that left her both hollow and more determined than ever.

"Look," he said. "You have your vision of beauty. I have mine."

They stepped out from under the protective canopy of the woods and back into the bright clarity of the sun where there was no place to hide.

"Turning this place into something that will reconcile even a bit of my past is what I find beautiful."

And there it was. The ugly truth.

His endgame was to level his past as some sort of payout for his pain, while hers was to ensure life and preserve her memories. Two sides of a coin, a yin and yang—and she couldn't blame him.

But she couldn't be blamed either.

Nodding toward his crew, she sighed. "You better get back to work."

"You're going to be okay, Larkin."

Her name slipping through his lips seemed to make promises whispered on humid nights and late, lazy mornings. Promises her body would be happy for him to keep. Steeling herself against the unwanted attraction, she lifted her chin. If her plan worked, she would be okay. But he might not be.

"So are you, Ryker."

~

*O*nce in her car, Larkin watched him with the men, their heads bent over the large land map. They could plan all they wanted— she had one of her own.

She headed toward home through an early afternoon mist. The thought of going to visit her parents as she'd originally planned seemed too daunting now. They'd understand after the day she'd had.

The mechanics of driving through the trees and their speckled light usually soothed her, nerve ending by nerve ending. But it wasn't working today, not after facing such disappointment. She traveled the few miles along the coastal road between her home and the Cape, shutting out the surfacing memories until she couldn't. Eyeing the narrow, open grate bridge with its unforgiving steel sides, she slowed the car.

And wanted to punch her fists into the steering wheel.

She eased her car onto the shoulder of the road, focusing on the vibrating edge markers, and threw it into park. It had taken her a long time to drive the same route, but the alternate way home was an hour around the city. After the first year, she'd felt ridiculous and forced herself to deal with it. It wasn't easy, but day by day she drove over the bridge without breaking down. Now she wished she'd taken the other way.

Her husband, John, had agreed to pick Archer up from the Cape to save Larkin the drive back home. She'd planned on spending some time with her best friend Blayne in town, searching for the perfect location for Blayne's artisanal shop—a plan she regretted now and would forever.

John had a temper and it was never more apparent than when he was behind the wheel. She'd warned him over and over again to calm down, take a deep breath, especially when Archer was in the car. He had a habit of snapping from zero to sixty, but he'd always told her it was his passionate nature, that it was under control.

She'd been a fool to believe him. No one had control over a bad temper they wouldn't admit to having. She had trusted their son in his care because he was Archer's father; because she was supposed to. Her throat tightened as if the memory were an anaconda wrapped around her neck.

John and another driver had jockeyed for position to enter the small bridge just north of the North Cove with such ego-laden focus, neither had made it. They couldn't even have been going that fast, but stormy weather and stubborn pride had made the perfect conditions for devastation.

A shudder wracked her frame and she covered her mouth with a trembling hand. She sniffed then pulled in a deep breath, resisting the urge to let the full onslaught of tears come.

She worked hard to remember that even with the finality of it all, Archer's contagious giggle persisted its echo in her heart. She was so thankful that during his short life, he'd had a reason to laugh fully and often. It gave her something to hold on to when she found herself struggling to get through each day.

It was time to pull up her bootstraps, focus, and save his Cape. It seemed Maxine had trusted the land in the hands of her grandson. Probably because she felt she should.

And he was driving *it* straight into a steel bridge.

Bracing against the memories, she pulled back onto the road and worked on a smile through the winding, wooded route back home. She pressed her foot on the gas pedal a little harder as she made a mental list of what she had to accomplish in a very short period of time. If Ryker's stubborn determination was any indication, he planned on moving fast.

Which meant she had to move faster.

The weight of grief subsided and was replaced with small flutters of possibility. The finger of land wasn't the kind of place to simply visit but rather move into and make it home. It made visitors want to run through the large Victorian house and pick a room all for themselves. It inspired poetry and music and epic love stories. It felt more like home to her than her own did these days.

She laughed in the quiet of her car. Epic love stories, indeed. Everyone knew how they ended. Zelda and Scott Fitzgerald had been very good examples. At the moment, Larkin felt a bit like Zelda—so lost these days, she had to use a map to find herself. That kind of baggage was no good to anyone.

The Cape, the well, they called to her, not only because they were the last place her little boy had laughed, but also because they spoke of happier times when her heart overflowed with possibilities for the future. When little hazel eyes peered at her so lovingly and a small hand slid into hers so trustingly. She rubbed her locket between her fingers. Archer always knew his mommy would keep him safe.

The sweet scent of his shampoo hit hard and her heart squeezed painfully in her chest. How many times had she kissed his head, rubbed her lips against his silky hair? Smiled into eyes so much like her own? Every day? Every hour?

Until she couldn't.

Until her reality, her existence, changed in the blink of an eye, in a moment of reaction, a moment when two men let anger replace reason, and in the end, no one had gotten anywhere.

Well, that wasn't true. Larkin had gotten somewhere, a place in her life she'd never wanted to be—a mother without her son.

She'd *had* the epic love story of her lifetime.

Tightening her hands on the steering wheel along with her resolve, she turned into her driveway with its view of the Cape's lighthouse across the waters of the North Cove. With the rare butterflies, the apiaries, and other significant flora and fauna, she was going to have it declared for conservation.

Ryker Van Buren wasn't building a damn thing.

CHAPTER 3

*R*yker tugged the zipper of his jeans up, not bothering to cover the yawn that stretched his mouth wide as he shuffled barefoot toward the door. The bell rang a second time, and he scowled. Scrubbing his hands through his hair in an attempt to wake the hell up, he promised he'd strangle whoever stood on the other side. It was seven in the goddamn morning and he'd yet to have a peaceful night's sleep in this godforsaken house. All he wanted was a solid twenty-four hours of brainless slumber. Was that too much to ask?

Yanking open the door, he grated out. "What in the hell do you wa—"

Maxine Van Buren brushed right past him. "You're lucky I didn't just use my key. But I lived with a man long enough to learn my lesson about catching him unawares." She gave Ryker's chest a pointed glare with an over-processed shudder.

Did his grandmother seriously just accuse him of masturbating? Talk about making a man feel like a boy. This was not what he needed when he hadn't even had his coffee yet, but if he'd learned anything about the woman, it was that if given one inch of rope, she'd take the whole coil, then hang him with it.

He joined her in the gothic-inspired kitchen and put a kettle of water for coffee on the large gas range. Ebony cupboards, boasting recessed, white-washed decorative edging ran from the floor to the white tin ceiling that echoed the large gleaming white, marble island standing proudly in the center.

27

"Clearly I wouldn't have my pants on if I was otherwise engaged."

She snorted. "Don't be crude."

"Me?" His brows raised. Talk about the pot calling the kettle black.

With a small tablespoon measure, he added scoops of a dark roasted coffee into his French press.

"Why don't you use the single serve coffee maker like normal adults do these days? I bought one just for you."

He shook his head. "And I'm sure it makes great coffee but I like the practice of using the French press. There's a process. Order. It centers me." He lifted the bronze coffee bean bag. "I just bought this from that new artisanal shop off of Van Buren Boulevard yesterday. Do you want some?"

"Yes, please," she said. "It only seems new to you because you've been gone for so long. That shop's been there for two years now. Eclectic Finds. Blayne MacCaffrey's place."

"Of course you'd know her." Grandmother knew everyone. And he tried to shrug off the weight of guilt from not coming home, but it had always been easier to have her come to him. Unfortunately, years of buying her plane tickets didn't ease the burden as he'd hoped.

She rapped her skinny knuckles against the top of the large island as she pulled up a black, grommet-studded stool. "Lived here all my life, of course I know. But even if I hadn't run across the adorable little shop myself, Blayne and Larkin are best friends."

The name alone sent a weird curiosity skittering across his skin. Clenching his jaw against the sensation, he remained silent and finished making their coffee. Anything he said would only invite more remarks from Maxine that he wouldn't want to hear anyway.

Her eyes grew wide with concern. Waving her hand at him, she demanded, "What happened to your side?"

"Oh, nothing to worry about. I got a little banged up trying to save Miss Sinclair's necklace before it fell into the well a few days ago."

"That was kind of you." She said it as if surprised and he rolled his eyes. "Have you been to Dr. Stanton? He'd love to see you. I'll call—"

"No, I'm fine."

"But—"

He lifted his arm to give her a better look. "See? Larkin patched me up onsite, whether I wanted her to or not."

A pleased smile curved her lips. "Sounds like my Larkin."

He grunted. "Well between you and *your* Larkin, I'm feeling a bit smothered. You do realize I'm quite capable of taking care of myself."

Maxine acted as if she hadn't heard the sarcasm in his voice at all and asked, "So she saw you with your shirt off?"

Gritting his teeth, he shook his head in a what-the-fuck manner. "What the hell does that have—" He stopped and finished preparing their drinks. On second thought, he wanted nowhere near whatever was going on in his grandmother's head. There was no telling what she might be thinking, and the woman came up with some of the scariest ideas he'd ever come across.

With two full mugs in his hands, he gestured with his chin. "Come on. You can grab me a shirt on the way and we can get to work. I know why you're here."

"So Larkin passed on my message?" Her undisguised curiosity gauged his response.

"She swung by yesterday. But even if she hadn't, a track suit is not your usual style for going out on the town, even if it is crushed velvet."

He thought back to the times they had visited over the years. Even without him living in town, they'd spoken on the phone and made regular plans to see each other. He may not have come back to the Cape for a long time, but he'd never stopped loving his grandmother. At every visit, she'd arrive dressed to the nines with her silver hair shining as bright as the rings on her fingers.

Smoothing her hands over the light gray jacket, she grabbed the hem and gave a purposeful tug. "Well, then. Let's get to work."

He made his way up the attic stairs two at a time, immediately swamped by memories from when he could only take them one by one. The air was stale and particles of history swirled in the rays of the sun shining through the slats of the large circle vents in each gable.

Maxine walked to the center of the large, open room and turned in a slow circle. "Lord almighty, it's been a few years since anyone's been up here. I probably should have dusted, but this damn house outgrew me as the years have gone on."

Ryker tried to look at the memories through her eyes but all he saw were his hiding spots during his father's drunken rages.

"What exactly do you want to do?"

She put a finger to her lips as she looked around. "Well, I don't want you to have to bother with a bunch of junk that has no meaning to you. We'll make a pile to donate, a few things I'll keep and put into storage, and if there's anything you might want, you can have it."

"I don't need anything."

She walked up to him, and he set his jaw. The concern shimmering in her eyes tightened the muscles along the back of his neck. A million different images flashed through Ryker's mind and he couldn't decide which was worse: his father's fist as it sailed toward his face, his mother's profile as she simply turned away and continued to knit in her rocking chair, or the hopeless sorrow in his grandmother's eyes when he'd shown up on the doorstep of the guest house with a black eye for the thousandth time.

She and grandfather had moved to the modest cottage when he'd come along, leaving the big house for them to make a home. Too bad his parents hadn't been better at it.

Grandmother had called the police more than once but he'd refused to admit what had happened. And though there had been an investigation and home visits from CPS, Ryker had been quite convincing. It was hard to land a conviction when the victim wouldn't cooperate.

His father had threatened his grandmother's life if Ryker ever said a word—and he'd believed him. His childhood had sucked. He didn't need to talk about it. He didn't need any pity. Maxine loved him and that was good enough.

Jabbing a finger in the air, he startled her. "I lied. I do want something. Your moonshine."

Her perfectly manicured brows snapped together so fast he had to smother a chuckle. Nobody screwed with Maxine Van Buren's moonshine. She'd been making it long before Ryker had even been a thought and perfected the aging process as well as a combination of berries and flowers that would make the devil himself sing hallelujah. He couldn't remember how many times he'd stood at his bedroom window, watching her and her North Cove Mavens drinking well into the morning around the backyard fire pit and howling at the moon.

A warmth rushed across his chest. Even though they'd been drinking, he'd always felt safe hearing their cackles and laughter outside. His father left him

30

alone when people were around. Especially Maxine's people. And for some reason, the moonshine was one thing the old man had refused to drink.

"In your dreams. That's going with me." She pushed past him toward the crates of her homemade stash. "You and Mitch were always stealing it when you were younger." She shook a finger at him. "Don't think I didn't know."

"Well, that's your fault for making it taste like freshly squeezed juice. You can't tell me to get all my fruits and vegetables and then get mad at me when I do."

She rolled her eyes. "Flattery and fancy talk will get you nowhere with me." Picking up a two-layered, beekeeper's hood with a collapsible veil, she turned toward him. "And don't think I don't know when you're in avoidance mode."

Swallowing back a sigh, he pulled out a box. "Look. I'm not trying to be a dick."

She raised a silver brow.

"Sorry, a jerk. But what's done is done. You love me. That's all that matters."

With a warm smile, she brought the hood close to her nose. "I imagine I can still smell your grandfather's cologne, but I know better. He never worked with the bees unless he was clean and scent free. He said it was the best way they could get to know him."

"That reminds me. You have a beekeeper working the hives, don't you?"

Her lips curved down. "Not since I started preparing to move. The expense didn't seem justified, and I certainly can't take the bees with me."

"But I think they're getting honey-bound. That can screw up the whole hive."

Brilliant blue eyes that saw too much and said even more held him in his spot. "Then take care of them. You know as much as any beekeeper I could hire. Your grandfather made sure of it. But I don't see what the point is. As soon as you start building, they're going to be destroyed."

He winced as a sharp, stabbing pain nailed him between the shoulder blades. "So you heard about that."

She was mad.

He couldn't blame her but the decision was his. Why would she sell him the Cape if she was worried about what happened to it? Shoving the guilt away, he cleared his throat.

"I'm considering a plan that can incorporate the hives. It may mean relocating a couple. I'm going to look into it."

She grabbed the bee suit and carried it over along with the hood. Pushing them against his chest, she said, "Here. Grandpa would want you to have them. Maybe working with the bees will help you remember what you loved about this place and keep those memories of your father at bay."

Placing her smooth, cool palm on his cheek, she tilted her head. "Have you seen him?"

"No. And I'm hoping to keep it that way."

She nodded then bent over to pull out a large trunk. "I hope so, too. He hasn't changed at all. How sad is it that his own mother avoids him?"

Sadness rolled into his gut like great boulders, leaving it heavy and hard. As much as he'd been hurt by his father, his grandmother had been heartbroken over her son. She and Grandpa had never understood where they'd lost him. But after a stint in combat overseas, he'd come back a changed man. And not for the better—a living casualty.

Ryker frowned. He'd always heard losing a child was the worst pain. Maybe that's one reason Maxine and Larkin had bonded so tightly. A vision of the woman's sweet smile popped into his head, along with that damned dimple, and he gritted his teeth against the inopportune tightness in his body. The simple thought of her had him imagining all sorts of ways to keep that dimple deep. All. Night. Long.

The doorbell gonged as if the hunchback of Notre Dame was working overtime, and at the same time, Ryker's text notification went off. "What the hell?"

He set his grandfather's bee suit aside, careful not to crush the netting on the hood, and grabbed his phone from his pocket.

Mitch: At the front door.

Ryker: Come in then, jackass. In the attic.

Sliding his cell back into the pocket of his jeans, he opened the box he'd pulled out earlier.

"You're not going to get the door?"

"It's Mitch. He's coming up."

She nodded in approval. "Good. He can help."

He and Mitch had gotten so good at staying under the radar to keep from having to work Maxine's cockamamie plans over the years that a U.S. Special

Forces team would be proud. Her plans had always traveled well past crazy and solidly over to insane. He couldn't count how many times she'd almost been arrested—how mortifying would it have been to spend time in jail over a flower heist?—or in the emergency room due to pride or obstinance. Especially when it came to her damn moonshine.

And every time, dressed, pressed, and ready to impress.

She could avoid all the trouble if she wouldn't sell it. But trying to tell her that was like trying to teach a lobster to dance.

He watched her flip through some old record albums with a dreamy smile on her face that promised she was thinking of years gone by. Probably dancing with Grandpa on Sunday night, or the large sit-down dinners she'd put on for their friends—which more than once ended with the moonshine pulled out of storage.

"You guys up there?" Mitch called from the bottom of the attic steps.

"Get up here, young man, and don't tell me you're still afraid," Maxine answered with a roll of her eyes and a huff.

Mitch ascended the stairs in a slow death march, each step echoing off the attic rafters. He had always hated the attic but braved it whenever Ryker had been in hiding. Mitch always preferred hiding in the woods. He'd say it was easier to run for his life if he ever needed to.

The two men went way back, so far Ryker couldn't remember when they'd actually first met. One too many hits to the head could do that to a guy. But what he did remember was middle school, when Mitch hid him in his room while Ryker's dad rampaged or how Mitch would talk his mom into having Ryker over for an extended weekend just to give him a reprieve from the hell that was his home on the Cape.

"I am not afraid of the damn attic." Mitch caught himself, sending a look of chagrin to Maxine. "I mean darned attic."

She waved a hand in dismissal and turned her attention back to her albums. "Since when do I care what the hell kind of language you use?"

Mitch sent a pained look to Ryker, but he could offer no help. Stepping to Maxine's side, Mitch kissed her cheek. "I'm trying to be respectful. You're getting—"

Maxine narrowed her eyes. "If you say old, I'm going to wallop you with this stack of classics."

Ryker's buddy backed away slowly, as one might from wild wolves. "Of course not, I was going to say...respected. Now that you're dating Judge Carter, I just thought—"

That got Ryker's attention. "Carter? Who the hell is Judge Carter?"

Maxine scowled. "I don't want to hear one word about my dating life until you have one yourself."

No other words could shut him up faster, but he'd use his connections to look into this Judge Carter guy. He didn't trust anyone when it came to his grandmother. Gold diggers came in all shapes and forms. The fact that he felt ridiculous even thinking it did not diminish his protective instinct in the slightest.

"Anyway, you know I'd love to stay and bullshit all day." Mitch quickly pointed at Maxine. "You said I could swear... But we have a problem." He shifted from one foot to the other as he turned toward Ryker. "Can I speak with you in private for a moment?"

Ryker stood from the box of puzzles that made him think of the well and a little boy and promises made. The well had never worked for him and it hadn't worked for Larkin's son either. "Anything you have to say can be said in front of my grandmother. What kind of problem?"

His buddy glanced at Maxine as if he might get sick, and Ryker swore the man was still as afraid of her as when they were children.

"Holy shit, man. Come on."

"No," Maxine interrupted. "I'm going to the kitchen for some water. No need for you guys to run off and whisper in private when I know how much Mitch loves it up here."

Mitch dropped his chin to his chest. "We'll be just a minute."

Maxine grinned, having enjoyed harassing Ryker's friend since he was born, and disappeared down the stairs.

The two men made their way out of the attic and into a wide hallway that overlooked the great room below. Ryker walked over to a large, striped settee, then turned around. "Feel better now?"

Mitch simply rubbed his nose with his middle finger.

"So what's this about?"

"Are you dead-set on developing the Cape?" his friend asked, clearly shifting into attorney mode.

"Sure as shit." Ryker shoved his fingers into his jean's pockets.

"What about Maxine?"

Ryker held Mitch's questioning gaze with a hard one of his own. "What about her? She assured me she was ready for a change, moving to town with a view of the square." A small itch formed between his shoulder blades, and he rocked back on his heels.

Mitch grimaced. "But I can't imagine she meant for you to sell the family estate off in pieces."

"I think she means for me to do whatever the hell I want with it. Besides, I've more than earned the opportunity to put my past to rest. And I mean to do so by making a shit ton of money for my future." He looped a hand over the back of his neck. "If I can just keep people from popping onto the property every other day." Larkin's beautiful face hovered in his subconscious. The thought of not seeing her caused a pinching sensation he neither understood nor liked one bit.

"Want me to put a patrol on the entrance? I've got some pull with the county police department."

That caught Ryker's attention. "Pull? Since when?"

His buddy grinned. "Let's just say the policewoman uniform fantasy is spot on."

"Not touching that with a 10-foot-pole, standing in another state, my friend."

Mitch laughed with a nod. "Smart man."

"No, I'm thinking about Larkin Sinclair. She comes to hike the property and visit the well."

"She's hot." Mitch offered, easily distracted by pretty, shiny things.

Fuck. She really was. Ryker nailed him with a hard look, all his efforts to rein in his frustration beginning to wear thin.

"Dude." An image of Larkin clouded his vision. She was gorgeous and off limits. "Single, yes. Available, not so much." He used the tone reserved for clients who wanted to jump on the newest investment trend without doing their due diligence. Partly patronizing, partly authoritarian, leaving most people mute and stepping back from him. But Mitch had never been intimidated by his size or his success, so his friend simply ignored the comment.

"Single means available. Think she'll ever head out to the Cape again?" The look on his face said he'd be there welcoming her with open arms if she did.

The hell he would. The last thing Larkin Sinclair needed was attention from

Mitch Brennan. Ryker loved his friend but the guy's attention span was non-existent. He jumped from relationship to relationship like the squirrels on the Cape jumped from nut to nut.

"If she does, you're not invited."

Mitch studied him with a frown. The look in his eye eased into something akin to amusement and he leaned back against the hallway railing. "Ahhh...I see what's going on here."

"Fuck you. There's nothing going on. She visits the old well that her little boy loves." He stilled. "Well, *loved*. He died."

"And you're going to tear it all down." His friend raised his hand to his forehead, making an explosion gesture with his fingers.

Ryker stared at Mitch, swallowing the impulse to punch him in the face. He already had enough on his shoulders, dealing with his grandmother and Larkin. He didn't need it from this jackass too.

Mitch pulled some papers from his bag. "Well, I hate to be the bearer of bad news, but your friend might get her wish. I sent you digital copies, too. Though, I figured you'd want to take a look right away."

Ryker grabbed the paperwork and flipped through the pages. "What the hell is this?"

"There's an emergency stay from the DEP on development due to an application for conservation submitted by Land for Maine's Future and Conservation. Apparently, this property houses some rare plants and animals that the tree-huggers want to protect."

"Yeah, my land falls just under the acreage requirements for a full analysis but I had my team include a study anyway. The information is all included in my application."

"Well, they're sending someone out to research the property to...double check, if you will."

Mitch's air quotes accompanying the words 'double check' left Ryker gritting his teeth.

"They'll prepare a full land analysis based on newly submitted evidence of the Cape as a sensitive ecosystem, and then the judge and the board of the DEP will rule on it," Mitch said.

"Goddamnit." Ryker growled. The money he'd already invested dinged bill by bill through his brain. Hell, his engineering team alone cost a small fortune.

Waiting would only mean more money lost and delay his chances of putting his past behind him. He wasn't sure which was worse. "Who's the analyst?"

Mitch shook his head. "I just found out about this. I've requested everything be sent to my office. The claim slid across Judge Carter's desk last minute. He used to be a judge working in environmental law but now he's the chairman of the board for the DEP."

Judge Carter? Of course it would be him. Theodore Carter worked for the Maine's Department of Environmental Proction. Ryker had seen his name a few times since beginning the process of pushing his permit applications through last winter.

The old Victorian's bell gonged again and Ryker hoped the damn thing would break from the sudden overuse. "No one even knows I've moved in. Who the hell could that be now?"

They wound their way down the stairs, then into the three-story entryway with its black-and-white floor tiles and deep eggplant walls. But Maxine had already beat them there. He called over his shoulder to Mitch as his grandmother opened the door open. "I need to know who the hell the analyst is and now. I sure as hell don't want a damn stranger traipsing around my property."

Larkin stood, toes flush to the door frame, with a wide, overly victorious grin on her face. Gone was the hurting, nervous woman he'd first met. The transformation froze Ryker in his spot as he took in long jeans that covered all but the tip of what looked to be steel-toed boots, a fitted white t-shirt that hugged her breasts in a way that made his hands itch to take its place, and a light-weight, navy L.L. Bean vest that shouldn't be nearly as alluring as he was finding it.

She waved a rolled document in her hand. "Well, it's a good thing then that we're no longer strangers."

CHAPTER 4

*L*arkin's heart slammed against her ribs as Ryker approached the door like an angry bear, his dark eyes skewering her with a look that had turned from confused to hostile in the time they took to dilate. She couldn't make sense of the excitement strumming through her veins as he stalked closer. *But, dayum, the man was hot.*

All she had to do was stand her ground. She wanted to give him the courtesy of granting her access to the property.

"You did this." He shook the papers. "Goddammit." He swung back toward Maxine.

It wasn't a question and it was more than an accusation. If she knew him better, she'd have sworn he looked hurt. But that was ridiculous. This was nothing but a business venture for him. It wasn't personal beyond building his bank account and getting out of town. A payout as a payback. She understood if he was angry—hell, she'd have been shocked if he wasn't—but hurt? That she didn't get at all.

"It's important. I tried talking to you about it." She glanced around him with a weak wave to her friend. "Hi, Maxine."

"Hey there, sweetheart."

Holding the papers out before him, he poked at the front page. "Did you know about this, Grandmother?"

She gave a delicate shrug. "I might have had an idea."

"Un-fucking-believable. This is my home." He swung back to Larkin, rattling the papers.

"Ryker." Mitch put a hand on his shoulder but was shrugged off.

With a swallow, she lifted her chin and dug her toes in hard against the cushioned insole of her boots. Of course, he wasn't happy, but this was the right thing to do.

She simply needed to get him to see it the way she did. His plans would destroy so much of what made this property special. Not to mention the damage to the town of Cape Van Buren itself.

"A home you have no ties to." She rushed on with an outstretched hand. "And I understand, I do. But this town does have strong ties. And there is so much good that can come from this place. You saw the animals yesterday." She swung her arm out toward the path she'd taken through the woods.

He frowned, the scruff on his face shifting with the action. It had filled out a bit more since she'd felt the bristly hairs against her lips, and she pressed her own together to remove the sensation. Unsuccessfully. Damn it.

"If you could just—"

"What? If I could just what? Give it away? Ignore my own needs? Once again, you speak so passionately about everyone's feelings but my own. It's so easy when you sit on the opposing side."

She reached for him, but as her palm settled on his forearm, he tensed. Dropping her hand, she tucked it behind her back, rubbing his heat from her fingers. "We don't have to be on opposing sides with this. We both want what's best for the Cape. Surely you can see that?"

"No, what I see is you wanting what's best for you."

She winced. It wasn't a good feeling to be seen as selfish in someone else's eyes, but selfish be damned if it saved the well. With a dip to her chin, she agreed. "You're going to see me how you see me. Nothing I can do about that. In the meantime, I'm here, and I have a job to do, so as a courtesy, do you have a preference for when I conduct my analysis? I have a lot to do and less than four weeks to do it."

His bark of laughter made her jump and her eyes skipped to Mitch and Maxine in question. Ryker turned and disappeared toward the kitchen.

She shifted from one foot to the other, trying to figure out what to do next.

"Come on in, sweetie. Ryker has no manners, and this lout," She shoved a bony finger into Mitch's chest, "...doesn't either. It's a wonder he didn't turn out better. His sister Mae is an angel."

He threw his hands up. "Oh, sure. Everybody loves Mae."

"Including you," Maxine said.

"This is not my house. Besides, Ryker's an ass when he's mad. I'm too smart to get on his bad side."

Maxine snorted. "You're not too smart if you're okay getting on mine." She tucked Larkin's hand into the crook of her crushed velvet-covered elbow and led her to the kitchen. "Let's get something to eat. These things are always better with a full stomach."

Thank God for Maxine.

"Get her out of my house." Ryker slammed a cupboard door, holding a mug in his hand.

"Oh, please. You'll get her a cup of coffee." Maxine smacked her lips in appreciation as she pulled a box of cupcakes, with a North Cove Confectionery logo across the top, from the refrigerator. "Only cupcakes worth eating. Lemon poppy or raspberry beret?"

Ryker's dark eyes narrowed as he slowly inhaled through his nose, and Larkin resisted the urge to smile at how powerless the large man was in the presence of his grandmother. He put water on the stove then yanked plates from a shelf next to the sink. Maxine's influence to be sure. He moved with a tight but easy grace from place to place, filling the space with his spice and a heat Larkin could feel from across the room.

She'd never seen anyone's cheeks flex with such rigor in her life. The action drew way too much attention to the hard line of his jaw and the area she'd kissed in her misplaced appreciation when he'd saved her locket. An area she wouldn't mind kissing again. She shifted on her stool, trying to block the images her mind had conjured up of his broad chest and chiseled abs.

Her fingers found the warmed metal of her necklace and rubbed to ease the inconvenient urge to touch him.

Clearing her throat, she smiled at Maxine. When she'd called with her plan, she'd been prepared for resistance, but her friend had surprised her by getting the stay on the property pushed through in record time. There were apparently a few fringe benefits to dating the town judge.

Things were looking up. Ryker had yet to ease the anger from his gaze, but she was still sitting in his kitchen and about to enjoy the best cupcakes in Cape Van Buren. She'd take each little win as one step closer to the big one. Her dad had always told her, "You can't eat an elephant in one swallow, you have to do it one bite at a time." It was an awful visual but the lesson stuck.

"What were you doing?" She directed the question to Maxine. Seeing the woman in a running suit was a first.

Ryker poured four mugs of coffee. She watched the hard ball of his bicep flex as he set the pot down. He slid one in front of her plate. "What we're doing here is no concern of yours."

Well, so much for her little win—and her pride.

"I'm giving Judge Carter a visit this afternoon and we'll see about your little game." He glared at her.

Frustrated by his rudeness and her damn libido, Larkin slid from her stool and rounded the island. She stood toe to toe to prove he didn't intimidate her, though her heart slammed in her chest, and all the air left her lungs. "This Cape is no game and it does concern me if your activities over the next few weeks get in my way."

He leaned closer until they were practically nose to nose. "I really don't give a fuck about getting in your way. This is my home."

Heat rolled off him, surrounding her with surprising intensity, and she swallowed hard. "Well, we'll just see about that, won't we."

His eyes darted to her lips more than once and she licked them without thinking.

He froze. "What kind of game are you playing?"

"If you two are finished with your foreplay, I have a life to get back to." Maxine interrupted.

They snapped away from each other and her chest heated to an embarrassing degree. She pulled in a breath, chastising herself in fifty different ways for losing her composure. This visit wasn't easing her way at all, only making matters worse.

"Teddy's already made up his mind and signed the papers." Maxine stood from her stool.

Ryker turned toward his grandmother slowly. "Teddy?" He asked with an eyebrow raised. "Since when is Judge Carter...Teddy?"

41

"Since I let him sample my moonshine." His grandmother winked.

Something resembling horror washed over Ryker's face; apparently, he wasn't in the know when it came to his grandmother's love life.

Pinning Larkin with a look, he pointed at the front door. "Get out."

"Ryker."

Larkin put out a hand. "No. It's okay. I'll be overstaying my welcome in the next few weeks as it is. The least I can do is give him some room to come to terms with it." She stared at him. "Because I am coming back."

She didn't like causing the look of betrayal on his face, but there was no way around it at this point. Grabbing what was left on her plate, she headed toward the door. She might have to leave but she was taking her raspberry beret cupcake with her.

She walked to her car, focusing on placing one foot in front of the other. This wasn't a game. She had to do something to save Archer's memory since she hadn't been able to save him. Making a mental list of what she needed to do, she ticked each item off her fingers with a deep breath.

Record specialized species.

Photograph and record habitats.

Investigate soil composition.

She continued until her breathing settled. The analysis was in the bag and the law on her side.

But a ball of tension remained coiled in her stomach. There was a very real chance her tension had a lot more to do with how thick the man's chest was and that damn irresistible hard line of his lips than his anger over her presence on the Cape.

Not one man had come close to piquing her interest in the past two years, and it drove her mad that all of a sudden her body decided to wake up hungry for the one guy she couldn't be with.

On a sigh, she shoved the cupcake in her mouth.

She'd simply resist the craving.

~

*L*arkin took his damn cupcake. She had balls the size of a damn lobsterman.

Ryker gripped his hands tight. Apparently, the Cape wasn't enough for the woman, she had to take his favorite dessert, too.

He'd kept his eyes on Larkin's perky ass until the front door closed but the vision didn't desert him just because she was no longer in the house. When she'd licked her lips, his dick had taken it as a personal invitation and rose to the occasion in a very uncomfortable display of eagerness. Especially with a kitchen full of people and a grandmother who used words like "foreplay." He shuddered.

Every time he caught Larkin looking at him, he swore there was something going on in her head. He'd be damned if he could figure out what in the hell it might be, though. There was something about her that left his body on fire, but any man would feel that way when someone threatened his home—and that was the story he'd keep telling himself, too.

He took a bite of his cupcake, forcing it down his dry throat. Then he shifted from one foot to the other, the soft sound of his bare feet on the tile audible in the stone-cold silence.

Mitch cleared his throat. "Well, uh..."

Maxine could stare at Ryker all she wanted. It didn't bother him in the least.

"Don't you act like you're mad at me, Grandmother. I'm the one who's mad at you." Ryker took a long swallow of his coffee, hoping to ease the discomfort in his throat. Ever since he'd been a little boy, she had a way of making him squirm.

But he had to win her back over to his side so he could get on with this project before investors caught wind of the delay. This was too important to back down due to some misplaced ingrained fear of disappointing her.

"I'll be mad at you any damn time you make me mad, young man."

"You're the one dating Judge Carter. And how the hell did that stay on the land get signed? What did you do, give Larkin a character recommendation?"

Maxine's lips straightened into a telltale thin line and her eyes shifted over his shoulder. *Aha!*

"You didn't." It wasn't a question, but a statement of disappointment. His own grandmother was working against him. What in the ever living fuck?

"Well, you need to fix it."

She brushed her hands off over her plate. "I never imagined you'd sell the Cape off in pieces."

He scrubbed his hands through his hair then leaned against the island top on his forearms. "Why *did* you sell the Cape to me?" The fact she questioned the decision now was like a knife in the back. What he wanted was never right, he was never enough.

She studied him quietly for so long he almost asked the question again.

"Do you remember when Janice would bring her flowers and Evette would bring her fresh berries for me to use in my moonshine?"

He'd loved popping the strawberries straight into his mouth without washing them first. Grandma always had a fit. He nodded.

"Even though we always had a garden maintained, you said their flowers and fruit were better because they didn't hire someone else to grow them. I thought if you got a taste of what it was like to grow something of your own from this place, then maybe you could begin to love it. You could make it your own." She tilted her head. "Regardless, it's too much for me now and I won't live forever. You're my grandson and selling it to you brought you home. Simple as that."

"But it's not as simple as that. You say it's mine, but you're fighting for the opposing team."

Maxine moved to stand in front of him. "There aren't teams, Ryker. I sold it to you. You will do with it as you see fit. But so will Larkin. She's fueled by the love of her son, and I won't stand in the way of that."

His gut tightened with an image of Larkin sitting in her home alone. It was hard to reconcile her as a widow and childless mother. *Way to hit below the belt, Grandma.* He braced himself against the rush of guilt. "But you will stand in the way of what I want."

She smiled and grabbed his hand. "I don't think you've given yourself a chance to really know what you want. You're not wrong, but she's not wrong either. Teddy asked me and I answered. Now it's up to you to make them see that your plans are better and why. If you're so sure they are, then you'll have no problem."

But there was no light in her eyes as she spoke. His grandmother didn't want him to sell the Cape. A heavy weight coiled in his gut. Once again, he was being held back by his past when all he wanted to do was step forward.

"And you'll still love me, no matter what the court decides in the end?" The question sounded pathetic. Goddamnit. But she was the only person in the world he ever felt desperate around. Losing her was unthinkable.

She smiled with a small shake of her head. "I may have put in a good word for Larkin, but after your grandpa, you're the love of my life. There's no getting away from that. I just want you to be happy. And if your plan gives you that, well, I can't fault you one bit."

All he saw was the truth shining from her eyes, and he pulled her into his chest. "I love you, too."

She sniffed then batted at the front of his shirt. "Enough, now. The attic won't organize itself."

Mitch slowly eased toward the front door.

"Not so fast, sucker," Maxine called out. "You're helping."

Ryker's six foot two, grown-ass man of a buddy hung his head and took the stairs one at a time.

"Dude. That's sad." Ryker shook his head as Mitch slowly raised his middle finger in a quiet but succinct *fuck you*.

"Does this mean Larkin has free reign of the land?" Maxine's tone sounded a bit too victorious.

"Hell no."

Mitch brightened. "You have no choice."

This time it was Ryker who gave the finger.

CHAPTER 5

*L*ate Sunday afternoon, Larkin set the breast-shaped, ceramic salt and pepper shakers back on the shelf. Why in the hell they'd caught her eye while she was putting together a house-warming-cum-apology basket for Ryker was way beyond her.

But there she was, checking out a well-endowed rack. Probably the same found on the kind of women Ryker dated. She glanced down at her own modest set and sighed.

"Larkin!"

Slapping her hand to her chest, she swung around, almost knocking the breasts from their perch in the Eclectic Finds artisanal boutique owned by her best friend, Blayne MacCaffrey.

They'd met at Cape Van Buren's Ice Festival a few years after Larkin had graduated and had been inseperable ever since.

"Frick." Her whisper was hard but with no direction behind it. Looking up and down the aisle, she tried to focus back on eyes framed by miles of lashes. "You startled me."

Blayne hid a chuckle behind her berry-colored lips. Her light eyes twinkled in delight as she picked up the salt shakers. "I called your name repeatedly but you were too busy admiring my breasts." She turned the shakers over in her hand as if studying their craftsmanship. "Not really what I thought you'd be going for when you said you were coming in."

Larkin returned them to their proper place. "Stop it. I was just looking at them, and not for the basket I'm putting together."

Blayne lifted one perfectly arched dark brow. "No? Then what is going on with the color scorching your cheeks and chest? Your skin is as bright red as mine is pale white. Damned Irish blood," she finished with a grumble.

Larkin glanced down at the v-neck of her shirt and wanted to moan. Damn tell-tale blush. Of course, Ryker had noticed right away. Damn the man. "It's nothing."

Walking past her friend, she continued to peruse the shop, hoping Blayne would let the question drop. The store was full of everything imaginable, as long as it was handmade. All sorts of home decor, tools, and luxuries, from soaps and lotions to wall tapestries and breast salt and pepper shakers.

Blayne was as eclectic as her shop with her love for all things vintage, a passion for kicking ass on the Van Buren Roller Beauties roller derby team, and being a champion of change with her savvy instincts in business.

Shaking her head, Larkin looked over a Scotch decanter set and only half listened to Blayne rattle on about her date from hell last night.

"Bleedin hell. You're this embarrassed over a set of boobie shakers?" Blayne asked.

Born in the U.S., she'd grown up here, then moved to her family's home in Ireland for her teen years, until she moved back again for a boy at eighteen.

Which had not worked out well to say the least.

Now that she'd been back for the last decade, her accent was soft—unless she was pissed—and her English better than most Americans with but a few slang words slipping through now and again.

Larkin frowned as she placed the decanter set in the basket she carried. One of a kind and hand blown on the coast of Maine. Ryker would never find anything else like it.

Blayne patted her forearm. "Because I've been talking to you for the last ten minutes and you've not heard one word. Because I've never seen you so distracted, not even when we were on the way to the hospital because Archer was bound and determined to be born before his due date." Her light green eyes flew wide in dismay. "I'm so sorry. I didn't think—"

And there it was. The heavy weight that both filled her gut and left her hollow. She reached out to Blayne, grabbing her hand. "It's okay. You can always mention Archer. You know that."

Blayne's lips trembled until she pressed them together. "I know, but I hate the haunted look in your eyes every time I do."

"I'm getting better."

Her friend pulled her in for a hug, surrounding Larkin in the scent of the ocean, sparkling with a hint of lemon and earth. Blayne always said the perfume made her think of her family's home in Ireland, a place she hoped to return to someday. "When?"

Larkin smiled, squeezed her back, and then released her. "That is the question." She pulled in a breath, allowing the tingling sensation of possibility to flow through her chest. "I needed to find something bigger than myself again. Ya know what I mean?"

Blayne fell into step with her as she browsed the shelves. "I do."

"Well, I think I've found it." Her voice was almost in a whisper as if afraid the universe might overhear.

Blayne slowed. "What's going on? Why are you making a basket, or rather, who are you making the basket for?"

"Cape Van Buren has a new owner from the Big Apple itself. I met him Wednesday."

"And you're just now telling me?"

She ignored the censure in Blayne's voice and continued. "Maxine's grandson, Ryker. Unfortunately, Maxine forgot to tell him I had made a habit of stopping by."

Blayne snorted. "Maxine doesn't forget anything."

"True." She'd think more on that later. Maxine hadn't been acting at all like herself lately. Some people started second careers, but apparently, she was starting her second life—in town. And dating for the first time in decades.

"He saved my locket but then he told me he's selling the Cape."

Larkin waited for the explosion. She couldn't always express herself well, so sometimes it was extremely satisfying watching Blayne. And her friend didn't disappoint.

"What the ever fuck. I will neuter the bastard. Who the hell does he think—"

"The new owner, CEO of Van Buren Enterprises, and proprietor of one incredible body." She frowned.

Blayne stilled and narrowed her gaze. "Wait a minute. Incredible body? How the hell'd you see this boyo naked?"

"Five-hundred-dollar Armani shirt. He wasn't about to ruin it for my eighty-dollar locket."

"This sounds like some introduction. When are you going to see him again?" She winked.

Larkin shook her head. Leave it to Blayne to turn meeting a man into a hookup. "No, no. Nothing like that. I just need to feel him out a bit because—"

"Oh, I bet you want to feel him out alright."

Larkin slapped Blayne playfully on the arm. "Ohmygod, Blayne...focus. I'm analyzing his land for conservation. Which means he can't go through with his plans right now and therefore thinks I'm the worst human on the planet." She lifted the basket. "What's the saying about bees and honey?"

"You hate bees."

She waved the words away. "I don't hate them. They hate me. Big difference. Anyway. It's just my way to butter him up a bit. At least so he'll quit glaring at me every time I'm at the Cape. I need to find a way to make him love it like we do. And I'm starting tomorrow, bright and early." Dark, intense eyes popped into her head and her chest warmed. This was going to be a problem.

Interest sparkled from Blayne's eyes. "First, that is amazing, and I couldn't be happier for you. Second..." She eyed the basket in doubt. "My inventory is one-of-a-kind but I don't think the most awesome Scotch swag in the world will make this bloke happy with you right now."

"I have to try something. He feels like he's under attack, but saving the Cape will be a gift. He just can't see it yet. I'm going early tomorrow with gifts and coffee. If I could just reach him. Make him see..."

"He's interesting, isn't he?"

Larkin scoffed. "What? No. Please."

A huge grin spread her friend's berry lips from ear to ear. "I gotta see this bloke. Wear something sexy tomorrow. Men can try to deny it all they want, but a little cleavage goes a long way." She grabbed the basket and carried it toward the checkout. "When do I get to meet him?'

Jogging to catch up, Larkin sucked in a breath and grabbed Blayne's arm. "No

49

way. *You* are not going anywhere. *I* am simply figuring out how to keep my time at the Cape from being a constant wrestling match."

"Wrestling with a man can be fun. You've just forgotten."

Larkin took a deep breath and shoved the visual from her head. "You are a pain in the ass."

Blayne swung around. "I'm totally am, but I'm also calling bullshit. Not about the Cape. I get that. But you so want to see this bloke again."

"I do not. I—" She stopped mid-sentence and stared as her friend, wiggled her brows, and pointed at Larkin's chest. She didn't need to look; she could feel the heat flushing across her skin with the mere thought of the man. He was so tall she'd had to look up to meet his eyes. Eyes she had felt travel the length of her body in a glance. And that mouth. Wide and generous. When he smiled, it set her stomach on a low, slow, delicious roll—unfortunately, the same thing happened when he frowned. What in the heck was wrong with her?

Lifting her chin, she moved to brush past Blayne. But a woman entered the store and Larkin's stomach dropped. She ducked behind a display tower of city landscape steins.

Her heart pounded so hard it clogged her throat and the heat spreading across her chest raced to her hairline.

Blayne said something but the ringing in her ears made it difficult to hear. Two strong hands grabbed her upper arms. "Honey, what is it? You're okay. Breathe," Blayne demanded.

She tried to pull air into her lungs. "It's her."

Light green eyes opened so wide the whites surrounded the iris like an ocean surrounds an island. "You're okay." Blayne's words were reassuring but her expression betrayed her worry.

Mouth dry, Larkin tried to answer. Her fingers were numb yet tingled with pins and needles. She needed to pull herself together. Breathe.

Blayne peaked around the tower. "Oh, bleedin hell." Always a fast talker and a faster thinker, she walked Larkin toward the back of the store. "Let's go to my office." She stopped suddenly almost yanking Larkin off her feet. "Dammit. Hold on. I have to run up and tell my cashier her break is over." She looked up and down the aisle. "Okay, wait here. I'll be right back."

Blayne took off toward the front of the store as Larkin used the foot-steps to count out the seconds of breathing in and breathing out. Slowly her shock subsided. Leaning back against a wall of pillows, she let her head drop back and clicked her fingernail along each zipper tooth on her jacket.

It had been two years since she'd seen Claire Adams. Ironic that their paths would cross so close to Archer's birthday—and not in a cool, meant-to-be kind of way. All interactions between them so far had been complete disasters. Too much pain to manage niceties, so instead, Larkin had tried to avoid running into her at all.

Someone rounded the corner next to where she waited. She snapped her head up and pushed away from the shelves.

"Okay, come on." Blayne grabbed her hand and pulled her toward the direction of her office.

"No. Wait." She dug in her heels. She'd been hiding from the woman for two years; looking out for her when she went to Bellamy Grocers or scanning crowds during the multitude of Project Community Unity events downtown. Seeing each other triggered the accident as if it had happened yesterday. Claire had been wrecked, losing her fiancé the night before their wedding. And so had Larkin.

The door chimes tinkled. "It's fine. She's left," she said.

Blayne stood on her tiptoes, trying to see to the front of the store. "Yeah, I think she did. Okay, come on. Let's get this wrapped up so you are ready for your special delivery."

The air quotes around the last two words had Larkin rolling her eyes and helped her ease from panicked to poised-ish. "Oh my God. You never give up." She'd had a few mini panic attacks since Archer's death but it had been over six months since her last one. They weren't too bad but always left her feeling shaken

"You're right. I don't."

Stopping, Larkin dropped her hands to her sides. "Thank you."

"You're welcome. And I'm not done. You need to eat. You were thin to begin with..." She gestured her hand up and down in front of Larkin. "But now I'm frightened by how frail you look."

"There is nothing to worry about. I'm fine." Larkin lifted her chin. She ate, but her stomach rejected things more times than not these days.

Blayne didn't let up and spoke gently. "I know you're still devastated, and I really hope your new project helps you find your way back to us. We all lost more than Archer and his daddy—we lost you, too."

That stopped Larkin in a way no other words could have. She hadn't been the only one to lose something that day. So many people had suffered. Still suffered.

Once upon a time, their weekends had been filled with boating on the North Cove, sunbathing on the South Cove, BBQs on her back deck with the gorgeous view of the Cape across the water, and sleepovers with Auntie Blayne. Larkin's husband had gotten used to having her best friend around all the time, especially since Archer adored her, and she'd offered to babysit for date nights. Blayne had seen all the good and all the bad and had still come back for more.

Larkin's mouth opened then closed as she forced down the knot in her throat. "I was never lost."

"Says you. When's the last time we picnicked on the beach? Judged at the annual Holiday Ice Sculpture contest?" She grabbed Larkin's hand and squeezed with a wink. "Look, I'm ecstatic this guy has lit some sort of fire under you. It'll be even better if you win and get laid in the process."

Larkin shivered. "Seriously, you have got to stop. The last thing that man wants to do is hook up with the woman trying to take his home."

"Good point. You may need to rethink this."

Larkin laughed.

Blayne pulled her into her arms. "I love you, Lark."

"Me, too."

The front door chimed and Blayne released her to greet the customer. "Good afternoon, welcome to—"

"I forgot my…" Claire Adams froze with her decorative bag raised to chest level and her voice trailed off as her eyes fell on Larkin.

Blayne's clerk walked up. "Here's your receipt, ma'am. Sorry about that."

Claire fumbled with shaking hands as she tried to stuff the receipt in the bag and nodded her head in thanks.

Larkin's heart wept for the woman; she knew all too well the pain she suffered. "I'm…" She wasn't sure what to say.

Claire threw her hand up. "Don't." Tears welled in her eyes. "At least you got to have your baby and your husband for a little while."

Larkin sucked in a breath and spoke without thinking. "And it only magnified my pain. How can you—"

"But you had them. You didn't have your dreams shattered before you got the chance." Claire wiped at a tear on her face with a mortified look at her hand and hurried out the door.

Larkin tried to pull in a breath and the roaring returned in a crescendo in her head. She blinked back the tears and swallowed hard.

Blayne wrapped her in a tight embrace, a look of sorrow in her eyes, as Larkin spoke through trembling lips. "No, I just had my dream shattered after holding him in my arms."

"Oh God. Lark, I'm so sorry."

Easing herself from the comfort of her friend, she sniffed and lifted her head. "I'm fine. Really. We're both hurting."

"Maybe, but she had no right."

"She has the same rights I do. It was both men fighting to take the bridge first, it was both men who careened their cars into the steel sides at the entrance. But it was my baby boy who paid the price. And Miss Adams and I were left to pick up the pieces."

She pressed her shaking hands together and pasted a very fake smile to her face. "It was such an awful waste, you know? It didn't have to happen."

"I know. It isn't fair."

Larkin twisted her lips in a wry smile. "We know life often isn't. How long have you wanted to go home?"

"This isn't about me." Blayne's face remained blank but she couldn't quite mask all her pain.

"Look. I'm fine. Just a little beat up for a second. I've gotta go. I'll call you tomorrow."

It was easier to be alone with her thoughts than to have to hear them spoken out loud. How many times had she listened to the description of the crash, listened to the explanation that her boy had died on impact? At least as often as she thought about it and pictured the gruesome sight in her mind. It was too much.

The look that had crossed Claire's face when she'd recognized Larkin had been like looking at her own reflection. They needed to find a way to move past the pain and live again. She stared in the direction of the woman's receding vehicle.

And the answer might just begin with Claire Adams.

Larkin waved goodbye. She stashed her goods on the passenger seat, got in, then closed the door. The sudden vacuum of silence hit her ears and she dropped her forehead against the steering wheel. Claire's words echoed in her mind. She was right in a way. Larkin's memories were torture but, at the same time, she couldn't imagine living without them.

She pushed back and looked at her wrists, then her hands, with their white-knuckled, boney grip on the wheel. How had she let it get this far? Her once-golden skin held a muted yellow hue and the striations of muscle she usually saw running the length of her forearms were replaced with sharp lines and hollows. But that was all going to change.

It was a day for new possibilities. Larkin relaxed her grip on the steering wheel. She'd taken action and set a plan in motion. One that included the Cape and living again—and she was going to pull Miss Adams along for the ride.

CHAPTER 6

*M*onday morning came way too early as far as Ryker was concerned. But he had a lot to accomplish if he had any hopes of keeping the news of the stay on his property from reaching the ears of his antsy investors. One whiff of instability would have them jumping ship.

And that he could not have.

So he was up with the seagulls just as the sun was peaking over the white-crested waves of the Atlantic, trying to find the energy to make coffee.

He sat, half-laying on the marble top of the island, with his face in his hands. A cup of coffee would surely revive him from a night of tossing and turning against the teasing sex dreams of the woman bent on taking his home. He had blue balls the size of Maine.

He had to hunt down Judge Carter at the courthouse and persuade him to drop the stay. Apparently, the man maintained an office on the business floor of the old building. For some reason that fact pissed him the hell off.

The doorbell sounded like it was ringing from inside his head.

"Goddammit."

He tightened the string on his sweatpants as he made his way across the cool tiles to the front door. *I'm going to strangle Grandmother's neck.*

Yanking open the door, he opened his mouth to tell Maxine just that and froze.

The subject of his dreams, with her full lips and creamy skin, stared back at him from beneath the brim of a trucker's cap. Her eyes dropped to his bare chest and widened while holding out a cup of coffee boasting the Flat Iron Coffeehouse logo.

"Good morning..." Her words trailed off on a gust of breath as she shoved a cup into his hand.

There was no mistaking the look on her face and his dick woke up before his brain did. Apparently, some parts of him didn't need coffee to function. Clearing his throat, he dropped his other hand casually in front of his sweats and tried to think of his grandmother, her friends, then a group of nuns. But with the color of Larkin's cheeks warming and her lips parting on an inhale, his body decided not to cooperate.

The fact her shorts showed off miles of toned thigh and her top revealed the swell of her breasts between the edges of her unzipped army-green jacket did nothing to help in the least. What the fuck was the matter with him? She was a widow and trying to screw him out of his plans.

"What are you doing here?" He didn't mean for his voice to be so low or gravely, but he was still attempting to straighten out his tied up tongue.

Pulling her shoulders back, she blinked a few times then breezed past him into the house. "I brought coffee and wanted to invite you on a walk this morning." She turned around to face him as he closed the door. "Before you say no..."

Smart girl.

"Since I have access to your property to perform my analysis, you'll feel more comfortable knowing where I'll be and what kind of work I'm doing. I don't want to hide anything from you."

She darted her eyes around, seeming to have trouble looking him in the eye. The idea that his naked upper half might leave her feeling restless was a bit of a consolation to the debacle going on in his pants. Unfortunately, the knowledge didn't help ease his growing discomfort. Quite the opposite. *Christ.*

He rubbed his chest on a cynical chuckle. "You don't want to hide anything? Like what, going behind my back to see Judge Carter and using my grandmother as a character witness?"

She had the grace to wince a little. "I had to do something. And you wouldn't even consider my offer to buy it."

He stalked toward her, pleased when she lifted her chin and held her ground.

Stopping close enough to see the individual yellow flecks in her eyes, he took a moment to absorb the tension that flowed between them whenever he was close, silently congratulating her when she didn't back up. Her cheeks still held their flush and her pupils dilated. He dropped his gaze to her lips, reminding himself of fifty different reasons why he couldn't taste them and why he didn't want to. Though he seriously could not come up with even one reason for the latter. Then, without a word, he sipped from his cup and headed into the kitchen. He'd bet his most valuable New York portfolio that her taste beat that of the coffee, hands down. And the coffee was fucking delicious.

"How's your side?" Her voice was breathless, making him grin.

He absently ran his fingertips over the scabs. "Sore, but getting better." Stepping closer, he raised an arm over his head and gave the large scrape a glance. "Your nursing helped. See?"

Her fingers just barely brushed the uninjured skin along the edge of his abrasion then dropped back to her side.

She swallowed hard.

Hell, so did he. The sensation of her touch sent a wash of goosebumps along his side.

Eventually, he'd take pity on her and throw on a shirt, but he liked her off-kilter, especially when she currently had the upper-hand.

"So you want to show me the Cape? You do know I grew up here. There's nothing you can show me that I haven't already seen."

With a nod, she sipped from her cup. "I know you think so, but let me show you the Cape how I see it. Please. I don't have to take up too much of your time, but..."

He went over the list in his head that was already being delayed and scrubbed a hand over his face. Hell, so much for hunting down the judge before lunch.

"Please."

"Fine. But only so I have an idea of what the hell you'll be doing on my property. And don't forget that fact, Larkin. This is my *property*. I should be able to do with it as I please."

"I know."

He sighed. "Then why are you doing this?'

Her gaze dropped to the floor and, with a small shake of her head, she raised her hands in a shrug. "Because I have to. I can feel Archer here. And this land is

special. Saving the habitat and endangered species found here will make a difference. It's important to this area. I know you can't understand that, but this is
something I have to do. I have to try at least."

He dipped his chin. "Fair enough. But I have to do what is right for me, too.
So don't get your hopes up, cupcake."

It was funny how the challenge washed the sadness from her face and
replaced it with an arrogant rise of her brow. Or maybe it was the nickname.
Good. He preferred that look. It was easier to fight back against her when she
wasn't reminding him that her son died.

"Cupcake?" She questioned him with a haughty lift of her chin.

"Call it like I see it. You stole mine."

She blushed and mumbled, "I did not. You offered. Besides, they're damn
good cupcakes."

Exactly his point. "Let me throw on a shirt."

"Yes, please."

"What was that?" He smirked, extraordinarily pleased by her unintentional
admission.

Her eyes popped open wide. "Oh, nothing. Just...yes. Of course. I'll wait for
you on the porch." She hurried past him and once again his eyes followed,
snagged by the sensual curve of her ass and the long lines of her legs. His body
snapped to attention.

The woman was going to be the death of him more than the Cape ever
could.

A few minutes later, he met her outside, now covered in a Metallica t-shirt
with running shoes on his feet. "Thanks again for the coffee. I've looked everywhere for a cup as good as Miss Shelly Anne's at the Flat Iron but never found
any. One highlight to coming back to town."

Shelly Anne Mills owned the local coffeehouse. She was one of the South
Cove Madams, which made her a direct rival to his grandmother and the North
Cove Mavens, but he didn't care. Her coffee was glorious.

"It is the best, North and South Cove feud notwithstanding." She giggled,
grabbing the towels and Windex at her feet.

"What's that for? Going to scrub my bad memories away?"

"I wish I could." She held his gaze for a beat.

If only. But he had a few ideas about how she could try.

"Did you leave the decanter set on my porch over the weekend?"

She studied the bottle in her hand, pretending to tighten the top, but the blush creeping up her neck gave her away.

"Why didn't you just knock?"

Tucking loose strands of hair back from her face, she shrugged. "I figured you needed some space. I thought it would be a nice peace offering of sorts."

"A nice peace offering would be to drop this conservation analysis."

She shrugged. "I thought you might feel that way but I hope you like the set all the same. It's one of a kind." Her voice lifted with a hopeful lilt at the end.

They made their way toward the tip of the cape. The stone lighthouse rose above them, its family of seagulls calling good morning overhead.

She pulled in a breath then sighed. "I love the salty morning breeze off the coast. Just look at all the colors." She dropped her supplies, and they picked their way carefully over the craggy rocks. "Over here," she called.

Her movements were sure as her muscles flexed to lower to a seated position on the flat surface of a large rock. This was not the first time she'd watched the sun rise off the Cape.

Settling in next to her, he caught her light scent on the breeze. It was clean and fresh. A bit of lemon but with a hint of something else he couldn't quite put his finger on. But it filled his head with visions of those legs tangled in his sheets, his scent mingling with hers, and he forced himself to focus back on the sun rising over the ocean.

"I used to come out here with my grandfather. We'd get up early to do his morning check on the apiaries. Before we made our rounds, we'd sit here, and he'd tell me stories from his time in the Vietnam War. Most were sad, some shocking, but I'll never forget how after, he'd put a smile on his face and move ahead into the day."

He could feel her eyes on him as he spoke. It had been years since his morning sunrise ritual with his grandfather had come to mind. The man had been his hero when his own father was anything but.

"You miss him."

He held her gaze until she looked away. Tendrils of her hair fluttered about her face under the brim of the cap. The breeze off the coast always did have a mind of its own.

"Of course I do. But I'm not one to live in the past. It's my future I'm trying to shape."

Pushing up from the rock, he offered his hand.

She hesitated then slid her soft palm into his. The sensation traveled up his arm and he clenched his teeth against it.

He stepped back, taking her with him, and she stumbled.

She fell against his chest, laughing. "I'm so sorry. I can run all over these rocks, and the one time I let someone help me, I almost knock him in the ocean." Her face was bright as she found her balance in his arms.

The idea of him falling in from the weight of her made him chuckle. Her frame was so slight it raised all his protective instincts, and the feel of her in his arms roused all sorts of other instincts. What the hell was it about her? Her sweetness appealed to him as much as her audacity with the conservation analysis frustrated him. And he was never one for roller coasters.

Her body pressed into his and he felt the push of her breasts and the cut of her hips all at once, then she stepped away, leaving a chill in its place. Another time, another woman, and he would have taken advantage of the opportunity and pulled her back into his arms to taste her.

She ducked her face as she made her way to the grassy, level land away from the water's edge. She pointed up toward the seagulls. "Did you know that seagulls are attentive parents? The mom and dad mate for life. They take turns incubating eggs and feeding and protecting their chicks." Her ass lifted high as she picked up her towels and Windex.

He should look away, but fuck. Scrubbing his fingers through his scruff, he focused on the spiraling design of the stones forming the cylindrical shape of the lighthouse.

"Did you know that seagulls sometimes eat younger members of the species? 'Cause I don't think cannibalism is a compelling argument to keep me from developing the property."

Her face blanched. "Ohmygosh. You are awful. I was not trying—"

"The hell you weren't." He chuckled and followed her up the stairs. Her calf muscles tightened to a little ball with each step, pulling him along like he was on a leash.

They wound their way through a living room then a kitchen followed by two bedrooms until they reached the ladder leading to the lantern room. He'd always loved the little home inside the lighthouse. His grandfather's best friend, Henry, had lived there for years, even after the need for a lighthouse caretaker had passed. And once it sat empty, Ryker had only made the mistake of hiding from his father in the lighthouse once. There was no place to hide once you made it to the top.

The beating he'd received that night had made it hard to navigate the stairs back down. It was difficult to see when your eye was swollen closed. His fingers curled into fists, but he forced himself to shake them out along with the ugly memory as he stepped next to the large Fresnel lens. It dated back to before he could remember, but the shine from the glass assured him it was being well taken care of.

"Wow. I've always loved this view. Archer would always tell me he could see the whole world from up here. I can see him clear as day, staring out the window, a huge grin on his face, and Puzzle squirming in his arms."

She sprayed one of the many windows that provided a three-hundred-sixty-degree view of the ocean, his home, and the town.

The dreamy smile on her face turned her lips up in a gentle curve that left a shallow dimple in her left cheek as she scrubbed at the glass.

"What are you doing?"

She grinned at him over her shoulder. "Archer and I used to help Maxine wash the windows on our visits. Keeps the view crystal clear."

He grabbed a towel and stepped alongside her.

She squirted the window in front of him then continued with her work.

He shifted his gaze to the ocean. It was breathtaking, and in any other light-house, he might enjoy it. He scrubbed the window she had sprayed, and his gaze followed the line of the coast from south to north. It was beautiful. "Didn't grandmother hire someone for maintenance?"

"The groundskeeper helped out but he already had so much on his plate. The lighthouse isn't active as far as the Coast Guard is concerned anymore, but she liked to keep the light burning. It helps that it's a stationary lens. Less upkeep. No mercury." She handed him the Windex then ran her fingertips over the ridges of one large lens, leaving his body to tighten as he imagined those hands on him.

He took the bottle, squeezing just a little too hard and squirting a stream of blue liquid onto the floor.

She eyed the spot on the concrete that now looked like a Rorschach inkblot test, then focused on him before turning her attention back to the waters of the North Cove.

"The building itself has been maintained just as well as the house. She used to have her lunch out here at times, and once in while she and her Mavens have had some of their slumber parties here during the summer."

Oh, he remembered. It secretly warmed his heart that his grandmother kept up such antics, but he wasn't telling Maxine that. She'd find some way to use it against him. But he remembered seeing her profile dancing around with a lampshade on her head more than once as a kid.

And it gave him an idea.

"And she lit the lamp every evening for a long time, but recently scaled back to bad weather nights. I loved seeing the glow from my house. Made me feel less alone. It's been dark since she moved to town." She frowned.

"Well, that is something I can fix."

"Really?"

The possibilities rolled about in his head. It would be a great asset to the planned community of the Cape. He'd rent it out for guests of community members, for weddings, graduations, and the like, and the money could go back into the grounds for upkeep and operational costs.

"Absolutely."

Not to mention, the view of the town would entice visitors to check it out, which was always good for the economy. Judge Carter would love that. "Thank you," he added and didn't even try to cover up the smugness dripping from his words.

She narrowed her eyes. "For what?"

He chuckled in answer and rubbed his hands together. She nudged him in the side with her elbow, making him wince.

She shot her hands out, dropping her supplies. "Oh shit. I'm so sorry."

"Why do I get the feeling that you're going to cause me a lot of pain before this is all said and done?"

She studied him then dropped her hand gently against his ribs. The heat of her palm burning through the fabric of his shirt made him want to pull away in self-preservation, but nothing short of a hurricane was moving him from her touch.

With a whisper, she said, "I really don't want to hurt you. I can tell you've already experienced enough to last a lifetime."

Her scent wafted about, slowing down his brain. She moved to step away, but his hand slid over hers, holding it in place. Shifting closer, he ran his eyes over her face then he took off her cap.

Her breath hitched and her eyes dilated into dark orbs with a bright green halo but she didn't move away. Heat radiated in the space between their chests like a bridge of possibility.

Seconds ticked by. His heart slammed in his chest and his mouth watered with the thought of brushing his lips against hers.

"Then don't." He leaned closer.

And she yelped.

Jerking away, Ryker tried to assess what the fuck had just happened but the blood rushing through his head and other parts of his body left him dazed and confused.

"What in the hell?"

She swatted at the air. "I'm sorry."

A light buzzing met his ears and two bees flew around their heads then off through a cracked window.

"They may have made a nest. They wouldn't need to but we saw the other day that their hives are overfilling."

Larkin hopped around the railing to the other side.

"Whoa, be careful. You're going to go over and that fall will be a hell of a lot worse than a hundred bee stings."

"Says you." Her eyes were wild as she rushed to the top of the ladder.

To her credit, she tried to pull in a calming breath, but a bee buzzed past her head and she muffled a scream behind her hand.

Making his way around the railing, he wrapped his arms around her waist. "Come on. Let's get you out of here."

With strength that always surprised him, Larkin gripped his arms like a vice and moved in step. She squirmed against him in her attempt to avoid the bees as he maneuvered the ladder to the top floor.

Her elbow caught his side and he grunted. "Calm down."

"I'm trying."

"You're going to get us both killed." He shifted her weight until she was over one shoulder then used the railing to navigate the stairs. He'd bet a month's salary she'd be pissed later, once she had a chance to reflect on the situation, but right now he had to get her down the stairs without getting them both killed.

Unfortunately, the bees *were* pissed and a few more joined the crew. She hid her face against his back at one point, then tried to climb down, swatting at the air in blind defense. Thank God, she wasn't more robust, or they'd have met their demise at the bottom of the lighthouse.

"Quit squirming." He breathed through each kick of her legs and swing of her arms.

"Get me out of here."

Finally, he pushed open the door and deposited her on the ground, where she immediately bolted away. She ran halfway across the grass between the lighthouse and the waters of the north cove. Turning toward him, she struggled for breath, her hands on her knees. "Why are they so mad?"

He glanced back toward the top of the lighthouse, hiding his grin. "I need to check all the boxes. I'm not exactly sure, but I have an idea."

With her long hair blowing around her face and her jacket hanging off her shoulders, she looked like she'd lost a fight standing or maybe won one between the sheets. His body liked the second idea a lot better.

"Are you okay now?" he asked, walking toward her.

"Don't you dare laugh at me," she demanded.

He placed a hand on his chest not bothering to suppress his humor this time. "Never. Now tell me. You okay?"

Larkin nodded but she still had a wild look in her eyes and her lips turned down at the corners. It stirred something inside of him. He wanted to scoop her up and hold her tight. Soothe away her worries. Which was a problem, just like almost kissing her had been. He needed to pull his shit together. Though her fear of bees was ridiculous, he found it oddly endearing. She'd stood up to his raging about like an ass on Friday, then run from a tiny insect today.

"Thank you for the gift."

Her eyes wavered but stayed on his. "You're welcome."

"Still love the Cape?" he teased.

She scowled. "It's everything to me."

He held her gaze. "But it's everything to me, too."

CHAPTER 7

*L*arkin tried to shake the image of full lips and a day's facial scruff from her brain as she pulled up a few loose weeds then tossed them into a pile along the edge of the North Cove Garden, but it wouldn't let go. With the back of her hand, she shoved her hair from her eyes and leaned back on her haunches. At least the garden was coming along. Once they finished grooming it, the magic would start, and the South Cove Garden wouldn't stand a chance.

She'd count it as a win. By the end of the day, she planned for her second win to be cataloging the butterflies, lizards, and bees she'd seen with Ryker last week —hopefully without running into the man himself. She needed a chance to process her reaction to him in the lighthouse. If the bees hadn't swarmed, she'd had every intention of leaning into those full lips of his and finding out if they felt as amazing as they looked.

After her ridiculous tantrum, however, there was no way that opportunity would ever come again. Men didn't lust after women who ran from bees like a toddler. In the end, it was probably for the best. She had a job to do, and that job was stopping the man in question from selling his home. Not jumping his bones. She didn't have time to screw around with someone like Ryker.

The three remaining weeks she had to perform her analysis would go by fast, but it gave the ladies of Cape Van Buren way too long to speculate on her every move.

Blayne, cute as a pin-up model in her striped tube top and overalls with her dark hair wrapped up in a bandana that sported yellow chicks, gaped at her with her red-painted mouth hanging wide open.

"What are you staring at?" Larkin glanced down at the front of her coral "love" t-shirt and green cargo shorts, an awful feeling of dread rising in her gut. Had she said all that out loud?

"Don't play dumb with me. You don't get to announce Ryker almost kissed you then act like nothing happened," Blayne whispered with feeling.

"What was that, honey?" Janice, Maxine's best friend and the unanimously-voted Garden Queen, crawled closer on her hands and knees, her red curls bouncing about her face. That woman had a nose for news and eyes for details. No bloodhound in New England had anything over Janice Brennan.

Heat raced up Larkin's chest. The last thing she needed was any news of this getting back to Maxine. That would be her second fail in two days since her whole plan yesterday of making Ryker fall in love with the Cape crashed and burned in a fiery blaze of bees and mortification.

She shook her head. "Oh, nothing, Miss Janice. I was just telling Blayne that I stopped out at the Cape yesterday to set up my schedule to do my analysis and I caught Ryker just as he was heading to town."

Her friend nodded with a look of impressed approval and mouthed *nice* behind Janice's back.

"What's this? You were spending time with Ryker yesterday?" This came from Evette Kingsley, the owner of North Cove Confectionery and cupcake maker extraordinaire. She was tall and thin and had always reminded Larkin of Popeye's wife, Olive Oyl. The interest in the women's faces would have been comical if they'd been focused on someone else.

Larkin stood, brushing soil from her pants. "Ladies, the only reason I'll be going to the Cape is to work on getting it declared as conservation land. Period."

"Oh, yeah. Mitch was telling me all about that." Janice nodded. "Ryker's pissed. Can't really blame him." Then she shrugged. "That boy has been dealt more than his fair share of pain out on that Cape, as much as I love it myself."

Guilt wound its way tightly along Larkin's shoulders. She didn't want to hurt him but she didn't want him to destroy the precious spot either.

"And from what Mitch says, he's got a wicked smart team behind him. So watch your back, sweetie." Her lips dipped down at the corners and she rubbed Larkin's arm. "What are you going to do if the court decides in his favor?"

A heavy dread filled her stomach. The idea of losing the Cape, losing the well, felt like losing Archer all over again. Tears stung the back of her lids but she blinked them away. Janice was right. As hospitable as Ryker may or may not be, she could not let down her guard.

She'd forgotten he had a whole arsenal at his disposal. The only thing she had was Maxine's character reference and the law. And the latter was only temporary.

Evette tsked. "This is the most drama we've had since Shelly Anne tried to say her coffee was better than mine."

Janice, Blayne, and Larkin looked everywhere but at Evette, pretending not to hear her. Picking up a yard bag, Larkin shoved handfuls of weeds into it. "Look, it would help a lot if you ladies keep the whispers of any of this to a minimum. The last thing I need is the town getting involved. I just want to protect the Cape."

Maxine walked up. "Oh, honey, if you wanted to keep this quiet, you should have never talked to Judge Carter. That man gossips more than a salon full of blue hairs."

"Maxine! You're…"

The silver-haired fox nailed Blayne with a look. "I'm what…exactly?"

Waving her hands helplessly in front of her chest, Blayne glanced at Larkin.

Stepping between them, Larkin kissed Maxine's cheek. "Dating the man."

"Ha! Dating him doesn't mean he's perfect, just that he has good taste."

"I'm just saying this is a sensitive topic. I don't want Ryker to have to hear about it when he comes into town. He's mad at me enough as it is."

"Almost kissing you doesn't seem mad to me," Blayne said then slapped her hand over her mouth.

All the blood left Larkin's extremities. What in the hell was wrong with her friends these days?

Maxine's eyes brightened with way more interest than there should have been. "What's this?"

Larkin threw out her hands. "Nothing. That is *not* what happened. He merely helped me escape some bees." She set the yard waste bag at the edge of the garden. "I've got to go. There are a few supplies I need to pick up before heading out to collect my data."

"Condoms?" Janice asked in an innocent tone, then let loose a cackle of laughter, taking Evette and Maxine along with her.

"You guys!" Larkin cried. She hadn't even thought of sex in over two years—well, she hadn't before meeting Ryker anyway—and the idea that these ladies had her jumping into his bed unsettled her in more ways than she could handle.

Maxine slapped her friend on the back and laughed. "Oh, Janice. I like the way you think."

Larkin blinked twice. "Maxine, he's your grandson." What was happening? She wanted to silence the gossip not cause more.

"Exactly." She templed her fingers, tapping them together as if concocting a diabolical plan.

Larkin had no idea what had gotten into her friend lately. Well, besides a new lease in town and on life. At least someone was getting lucky.

She had to get away from these women before they said anything worse—if there was such a thing. "I have to grab supplies for soil analysis and water tests." She shook her head. "I'm going over to Get Cookin' for some storage containers." She rebelled at having to explain, but with the way these ladies rolled, there'd be gossip about registering for her wedding if she wasn't careful. They had opinions about everyone, some more factual than others.

Blayne pulled off her work gloves. "Want some company?"

"Because you've been such a big help so far?" Larkin glared at her.

Evette stepped in front of them. "But we're not done weeding and pruning. The Garden Festival is in two weeks. We have to win back our rightful place in first place from the South Cove Madams. I'm sick of them parading around with their medals when they come in for cupcakes."

"They won fair and square last year." Blayne reminded her.

Janice snorted. "There is nothing fair about sabotage."

Larkin waved and stepped onto the sidewalk. "I can help later but I have to get out to the Cape before dark."

Maxine, Evette, and Janice were back in the thick of the garden before Blayne even caught up.

"You don't have to come with me."

Blayne laughed. "Please, you're doing me the favor. I need to get to the rink today. Besides, those three scare me sometimes."

"That's because you're smart." Larkin locked eyes with her. "Usually."

"I'm sorry. I don't know what came over me." She nudged her. "But for the love of god, tell me what the bleedin hell happened."

Larkin groaned. "I don't know." She shrugged as they crossed over Garden Parkway NW, then Garden Parkway SE, to the sidewalk leading to the kitchen supply store. "We were just talking and I mentioned that I wasn't trying to hurt him."

"Oh, that's your first mistake. Don't let him see any weakness, any softness. He'll use it against you. I'm sorry to say it, but this is war, Lark. You have to treat it as such."

"But it doesn't have to be. I don't want it to be. I just want to save the Cape, to be able to continue going to the well." Her chest tightened. "I can't lose this tie with Archer. I had him for such a short time as it is."

Her friend rubbed her shoulder. "Then don't. Don't let him win. What happened to him as a boy was brutal, but that was his father, not the Cape."

"Yeah, but try telling him that."

Blayne was right. Staying on her toes with Ryker and his team was paramount. If she gave even a little, they'd bury her. She had to stay focused; she had to collect her data. Science would win every time as long as she gave it the effort it deserved.

She made quick work with her purchases in the supply store then joined Blayne back out on the sidewalk once again, checking her phone with a frown.

"What's going on?" Blayne asked.

She gave a non-committal grunt as she slipped the phone into her pocket.

They made their way down Van Buren Boulevard toward the Flat Iron Coffeehouse. "Let's grab a quick espresso, then I have to organize my plans and head over to the Cape before Ryker locks the gate."

They passed ETA, the local entertainment and travel agency, then Delizioso, Cape Van Buren's always-busy and always-mouthwatering Italian restaurant. Both women breathed in deep through their noses.

"God, maybe we should skip the Flat Iron and do tiramisu at Delizioso's."

Blayne clamped her arm tight, imprisoning Larkin's to her side. "We're going to Flat Iron. And you're explaining yourself. You're hiding something. I can smell it." She cut a cat-eye lined look at Larkin.

Larkin led the way inside Flat Iron and back to their favorite corner with two navy velvet arm chairs. Sinking with a sigh, she brushed at the leg of her cargo shorts.

"Quit stalling." Blayne gave her a pointed look.

"I have to do something." She checked her messages once more and the time. Her day was rapidly disappearing. If she didn't get out to the Cape soon, she wouldn't have the sunlight necessary to see in the woods. And even if every square inch of the property was ingrained in her mind, she was not traipsing through the woods in the dark.

On a deep inhale, she confessed. "I've been trying to reach Claire Adams. To talk to her. I really want to find a way to help. But she hung up on me the first two times I called and then quit answering altogether." She shrugged.

Blayne pulled her bandana from her hair and shoved it in her front pocket. The look in her eyes was all kickass and very little compassion.

"Calm down." Larkin had seen that look in her friend's eye on more than one occasion, and it never ended well. "I understand why she's avoiding me, but I have to try. I don't need Mama Bear Blayne to the rescue. You don't have to worry about me, you know."

"I can't help it. You're my best friend. Besides, I can't let anything happen to you. You're my only grown-up friend."

Larkin grinned. "It's funny that in our thirties I'm your only grown-up friend."

"Don't add me to that group, I still have two more years. But think about it. We have Marci."

"So much drama." Larkin wrinkled her nose.

"Kate."

"Still lives with her parents."

Blayne tapped her chin then jabbed her pointer finger to the sky. "I got it. Victoria."

Larkin adjusted the package in her arms. "Is still wearing her tiara from winning homecoming her senior year."

"So weird." Her friend threw her a lopsided grin. "See? You really are it then. I have to watch out for you. I'm S.O.L. if anything happens."

Larkin nodded. "Yes, ma'am." She studied Blayne. Might as well detonate her bomb. "But we can also have Claire Adams, or we could in time."

"Now you're just mad." Blayne set her chin in the stubborn way Larkin had come to love.

"I've been thinking hard about it. She isn't coping with the accident any better now than when it first happened, and I've just turned a corner myself. I understand the feeling that tomorrow won't be any better. We have to help her."

"But she's been brutal," Blayne said. "Case in point, your most recent attempts to contact her."

"Regardless, we have to try."

Her friend looked at her hard then put up her hands. "I said I'd help with anything. I meant it."

"Claire and I aren't very different, but she doesn't see it that way. We've avoided one another like the plague when we could actually help each other finally get through all of this. Maybe even help other people."

"What do you mean?"

"If I get the Cape declared as conservation land, I want to start a community outreach organization. We could use the house as the center. One of the interests could be a coping or life-coaching kind of class. We could also do environmental workshops geared for kids and adults, art classes, maybe wellness classes like yoga."

Blayne laughed. "Who the bleedin hell are you and what have you done with my friend?" She reached over and grabbed Larkin's hand. "You're going from barely moving through life to sprinting in one week. Don't you think you've enough on your plate with the conservation?"

"I don't know. Yes." She shook her head with a nervous chuckle. "But, the idea came to me the other night at your shop and it won't let go. This is bigger than me. Just like the Cape. And I think it would help Claire."

"But what about Ryker?"

"What do you mean?"

"Honey, with your plan, you're not just talking about conserving the land, you've already moved him out of his home."

CHAPTER 8

*R*yker pulled the bee suit over his shoulders and slipped his arms through, ready for the escape he always found in beekeeping.

Breathing deep, he focused on the crisp, sweet smell of the freshly cut grass and the salty spray of the sea. On any other day, on any other cape, he'd be hard-pressed to find any better place, but his home was in New York with his work and very small social circle, and most importantly, no ties to his past or a beautiful, green-eyed woman in need of saving from bees.

Of all the ridiculous shit he'd seen. His lips pulled up at the corners. He loved the way she'd felt in his arms, the way she'd wrapped herself around him. The scent of her had clouded his senses and he'd come close to taking a thorough taste of her sweet mouth and anything else she might have offered right there at the top of the lighthouse.

And it would have been a terrible mistake.

Thinking about her was another.

Adjusting the now too-tight suit, he scowled.

He had more important shit to tend to right now. Mitch had warned him of some rumblings, so Ryker had put a call through to one of his investors. The group of them wanted to meet in person and assure themselves that he had a handle on the project. Of all the goddamn nerve. He hadn't built a reputation in New York for being the best land developer by fucking around. But this wasn't

New York, and over the years, he'd found that people liked to pretend their standards were somehow higher than those in the city.

Whatever made their dicks hard in the morning.

But there was no question from where true excellence reigned. It was a driving force in his decision to settle there in the first place. Not too close to Cape Van Buren, but not too far from his grandmother, and hard as hell to be successful. There was even a Goddamn song about making it in New York, for shit's sake.

He zipped the suit then, tucking the hood under his arm, grabbed his bag and retraced the steps he and Larkin had taken on Thursday. Stepping from the lawns into the woods was like slipping into a hushed cathedral. Every noise muffled, the lights dim, even his own breathing seemed somehow shallower and quieter amongst all the trees.

He'd added hummingbird nectar to the feeders a couple days ago and two little birds fluttered about like Larkin around bees.

The low hum of his striped little friends led the way and once he was just a few yards from the apiary, he pulled the hood over his head, draping the veil around his shoulders. The bees were gathering outside one of the hives in a small cluster. No doubt that inside, the frames were overflowing with honey, leaving no place for the queen to lay her eggs.

If he wanted to keep her in her castle, he had to collect the honey before it was too late. And not just the one box, but all the hives spread around the Cape. The investors would just have to wait.

He approached with slow, light steps, listening to what nature had to say.

Grandfather had always told him to be silent and let the world speak to him. If he was quiet enough, he'd hear its wisdom.

Well, he could sure as shit use some now.

Flexing his gloved fingers, he walked into the swarm. The low hum grew with the bees' interest. He was a threat until he proved that he wasn't. After two or three visits, they'd get used to him, but right now they were irate, as the higher frequency of their buzz relayed loud and clear.

With slow movements, quiet and calm, he set his bag on the ground and pulled out the smoker. He poured a little smoke along the cover, clearing the bees from the edge. Careful not to crush any of his little friends, he removed the lid then set it next to the box.

It was a nine-frame box and covered in burr comb. He carefully removed a frame, then scraped the overbuilt honeycomb clusters off the edges. Further inspection of the honey box and the brood boxes confirmed his initial assessment. The hives had overfilled. He wasn't more than a day or so away from these bees swarming and abandoning the hive all together.

He methodically worked through each frame, collecting them for honey extraction, then replacing empty ones for the bees to make or move more honey. The muscles along the back of his neck eased, allowing his shoulders to drop. The frequency of the bees' hum had settled into a quiet buzz, taking him with them into their little cloud of contentment.

Inside his hood, it was as though he were separate from all the bullshit that existed outside. The tension he'd carried with him all morning slid off his shoulders, leaving him feeling lighter somehow.

The lessons he'd learned from his grandfather came rushing back, making each move automatic as if he'd been there yesterday. Like seeing an old friend after years away and falling right back into a comfortable, familiar rhythm.

Next, he moved to the brood boxes. He'd collect the honey from a few of the brood frames and those he'd replace with empty ones. He scraped open the other frames filled with honey instead of larvae then replaced them. The bees would work at moving the honey to the super box, and while they stayed busy clearing out the brood frames, the queen could begin to lay more eggs in the empty ones.

Kind of like what he was doing with the Cape. It overflowed with painful memories. Parceling it out, turning it into a housing community would give it new purpose and make room for a future of memories that wouldn't constantly burn like the sting of his little winged friends.

He replaced the lid then stepped back to admire his handy work, feeling a sense of contentment for the first time since driving through the iron gates a week ago.

"Well, well, well. If it isn't the prodigal Van Buren child returning home to Grammy's house." The words were accompanied by loud, resounding claps from his father's hands.

The buzz of the bees increased as the ignorant man added a bellowing laugh to his show. Ryker stepped away from the hive and removed his hood.

A string of heat lit up the back of his neck and he flinched, but he refused to slap at the insect when the guilty party was standing in front of him. Tamping down his reaction against the burn, he walked away from the honey frames, forcing the man to move with him. The last thing he wanted was the hive to be disturbed any further.

Once he stepped from the protective canopy of the trees and out onto the groomed lawns, he swung around to face James Van Buren and tried to control the entwined thread of fear and fury that snaked up his spine. "What the hell are you doing here?"

He hardly recognized the man. Years of alcohol abuse and anger had drawn his leathery skin into a permanent frown and grayed his bushy brows.

"What am I doing here?" His father's tone dripped with sarcasm. "It's my home, boy. The question is what are you doing here? You scurried away like the damn pussy you always were years ago."

All the tension from the past week slammed upon Ryker's shoulders with a powerful grip. "Most wouldn't consider running from a monster cowardly." He gritted the words out between his teeth.

James let his head fall back in a peal of mocking laughter. "Monster? Says who? The big city business man? Is that why you've come home with your tail between your legs? If your grandfather could see you now."

"Leave Grandfather out of this. He was more of a father to me on his worst day than you ever were."

"Oh, fuck. Hail to Stuart Van Buren." James threw his hands in the air then performed a fake bow. "You think he was so goddamn perfect. You think he loved you? You were just a replacement. If he loved you so much, why the hell did you have to buy the place? Why wouldn't my dear old dipshit of a dad just leave it to you?"

Years of pain and anger and fear came boiling to the surface with such swift fury, Ryker felt the world go red as he grabbed his father by the collar of his shirt. "Get the fuck off my property." He shouted, hating the break in his voice. Hating the man for making him feel less than he was, hating him for making him lose his temper.

"I'm not going anywhere. And quit acting all high and mighty. You're nothing more than the scared little twit you were years ago."

Ryker seethed, staring into eyes too much like his own. "You can't hurt me anymore and you won't hurt Grandmother, either. I'm not a powerless kid half your size anymore."

"No, you're worse. You're a sorry, sack-of-shit, grown man."

Ryker tightened his grip, practically lifting the man from the ground.

"Ryker?"

His name spoken so quietly didn't make sense and he continued to stare at his father, seething at the nerve of the man for stepping foot on his land.

His father's eyes darted to the side and he sneered, "Call the police. Do you see this? I'm pressing charges."

Ryker shoved his father away, pleased when he stumbled and fell back on his haunches.

Larkin stepped close, briefly placing her hand on Ryker's cheek. Then she turned toward his father. Every instinct told him to throw her over his shoulder once again and carry her to safety.

She stepped toward his father instead. He grabbed at her arm but she shook him off.

"Call the police?" She asked quietly, cocking her head. "And why is that? From what I saw, Ryker was merely trying to keep an old man from falling."

What in the hell was she doing? His father was dangerous and she needed to keep her distance for her safety and his own sanity.

James snorted. "Keep me from falling? What the hell are you talking about, you crazy bitch? He attacked me and I'm pressing charges."

"Shut the fuck up." Ryker stepped between them.

Larkin placed a hand on his arm. "It's okay." Focusing on his father, she continued, "I don't think you'll do anything of the sort." She chuckled as she walked past Ryker and around his father's prone form. He wasn't sure what game she was playing. Who the hell was this woman and where did Larkin go?

"You see, I walked up while the two of you were conversing. Your son was trying to keep you steady." She tilted her head in an understanding nod. "So sweet of him if you ask me, but you yanked away and stumbled on your own feet, as one who drinks too much is prone to do."

She swung back to Ryker with a look of innocent nonchalance. "Makes sense, don't you think? And since the chief of police is my uncle, I'm sure he'll believe me over James Van Buren." She glanced back at the man with a raised brow. "You do have quite the reputation."

His father shoved to his feet and scowled. "You're fucking with the wrong man, young lady."

"Such niceties from this one." She dismissed him and looked at Ryker, merely gesturing over her shoulder with her thumb.

Ryker wanted to hug her and hide from her all at the same time. She'd saved him from making a huge mistake, but she'd also witnessed his greatest shame and the reason the Cape could never be his home.

James Van Buren.

His visit today was a potent reminder about why Ryker was selling.

One he wished he could forget.

*L*arkin wanted to pull Ryker into her arms and erase the haunted look from his eyes.

When she'd walked up on the two men, it was apparent there was a problem, but it wasn't until Ryker grabbed the old guy that she understood who he was.

After losing Archer, she had sworn she'd never let anyone hurt the people she cared about again. And she considered Ryker a friend. She'd been too little too late for her own son but she wouldn't fail this one. The very fact that it was Ryker's own father flicked a switch that made her feel ten feet tall and bullet-proof. She didn't care if he called her every damn name in the book, and the look on his face when she'd ignored his threats would hold her over for a long time.

"Come on." She put her hand out toward Ryker, but instead of taking his arm or hand, she merely directed him back toward the house. The last thing he needed was to be touched by yet another person who would only bring him pain.

He moved with her, vibrating with anger, but continued to watch over his shoulder

"Leave it. He'll be gone by the time you come back out. Let's grab a quick drink."

Once inside the house, she closed the door then joined Ryker in the front room. Dark navy-and-cream striped walls offset two plush chaise lounges covered in eggplant velvet.

He shrugged out of his bee suit then dropped to the lounge, grabbing a navy decorative pillow and holding it to his chest. In the soft afternoon light filtering through the drapes, she could almost imagine him doing the same as a boy.

When he swept his anguished gaze over her, she saw a man in pain. Silently, she approached the chaise. "Are you okay?"

She stood with her hands hanging at her sides and he trailed his fingers over hers. A wash of awareness raced up her arms.

He gripped her hand and gave a tug.

She plopped down next to him, a little closer than intended, and she sucked in a breath. Need shone from his eyes. But for what she didn't know.

"Ryker?"

He held her gaze, making her restless, but she stared back, lost in the stormy emotion she found there.

"Thank you. He's not happy unless he's hurting someone. But don't you ever do something so foolish again."

Ignoring his command, she stared up at him. "You know he was wrong, right? All those nasty things he was saying?"

He pressed his lips into a thin line then sighed. "He's dangerous, Larkin."

"Can I ask you a question?"

He tensed but nodded with one dip of his chin.

"Where's your mother in all of this? Maxine won't speak of her. No one does, really." Which was an anomaly, because the citizens of Cape Van Buren prided themselves on being fluent in everyone else's business and informing whoever wasn't.

He rubbed a hand over his face, breaking eye contact. She moved to scoot back a little, but he stopped her with a hand to her leg. The heat of his thigh already burned through her cargo shorts, but nothing prepared her for the slow turn in her stomach from the feel of his thick fingers and meaty palm gripping her.

"Stay."

No explanation of where or why...just stay. So she did.

But he didn't know what it cost her. No one had touched her since John had died. She hadn't wanted them to, hadn't been ready.

The thought of her dead husband numbed her. She was afraid if she looked too closely, she'd lose the tenuous hold on her temper that remained. It might not be fair and it left her with a little more than a lot of guilt but she couldn't stop it.

She was drawn to Ryker in a way that also scared her, that made her feel needy and desperate. Which was dangerous. Need resulted in vulnerability, which always ended in pain.

And her heart couldn't withstand any more sorrow.

But she stayed anyway.

"My mother wasn't strong. Not like the strength I see in Maxine…or in you," he said gruffly.

"I'm not—"

His eyes captured hers. "She wasn't strong and she mistakenly thought that there was no fighting against a man whose family owned most of the town. When he first started the beatings, he included her until she learned to sit in her rocker and ignore it. Then, when she couldn't just sit there anymore, she left."

"Oh, Ryker." Her heart squeezed painfully in her chest. His own mother watched his abuse then left him alone with a monster. How did any child get over that?

He stared at his hand on her leg. "Once I left, I searched for her. She's in Florida. That's all I know."

"I can't imagine. I could never—"

He put up his hand to stop her. "I know what you're going to say. You could never do that. You'd never leave Archer. But if you'd have asked her when she and my dad had first married, I'd bet the Cape she'd swear the same thing.

She grabbed his hand, resting it back on her leg, and slid her fingers back and forth over his knuckles. "Do you hate her?"

"I did. Then I didn't. I think I've come to the conclusion that I don't hate her for leaving, I hate her for not taking me with her."

"Ryker…" What could she say?

He leaned back against the cushions. "I'm fine. I think back to that boy from so long ago, and I'm pissed he felt such fear and pain. Like it wasn't me. Until I saw my father today. I can't stand that as soon as I saw that familiar look in his eye, the same old fear shot through me."

His fingers absently rubbed a small circle on her thigh.

How could she comfort him? How could she erase the look that haunted his dark eyes? She gripped his fingers and raised them to her mouth. Kissing each one, she held his gaze, watching his pupils dilate and drop to her lips.

"None of it was fair. You never deserved any of it. And it was not your fault."

Dropping his forehead to hers, he whispered, "I used to think if I'd just disappear, maybe he'd at least be nice to my mom."

She hesitated, the warmth of his breath washing over her lips, making them tingle in anticipation. Her heart slammed in her chest and stole her breath. And then she did the only thing she could think of to ease a bit of his pain.

She released his hand then slid both of hers up to hold his face. His scruff tickled her palms and she caressed the corners of his lips with her thumbs.

"Cupcake." There was a warning in his voice. But she didn't understand what he wanted or what he didn't.

The endearment shot a sizzle of awareness through her. With a small inhale, she leaned into him, capturing his lips with hers. Their plush heat was everything she'd dreamed of and warmth spiraled in an infinite loop.

He stiffened, letting her slide across his mouth with her own in feather-light caresses. Then a low, almost imperceptible groan reached her ears, and he pushed her back against the pillows of the couch, pressing into her, chest to chest. He swept his tongue along her lower lip and her nerves thrilled at the sensation.

"Larkin."

She opened for him and when his tongue touched hers a swift wash of heat rushed from her center out along her limbs. Sliding her arms around his neck, she pulled him closer still. He tasted like coffee and ocean breezes, and if he never stopped kissing her, it would be too soon. The weight of him against her was heaven. She wanted to rub her breasts back and forth along his chest until he took notice, until he eased the pressure with his hands.

"We shouldn't do this," he whispered against her mouth, then licked the sensitive skin along her jaw to her earlobe, which he captured with a small suck into his hot mouth.

"God. I know." She slid her hands over the large mounds of his shoulders and down his arms until she came to his hands gripping her waist. With a tug, she pulled one to her breast. Desperation filled her with a need to be touched, a need to have her pain eased as she hoped to ease his.

He closed his hand over her in a gentle grip and they both groaned.

His touch was a lifetime of experience she'd never had before. Overwhelming, terrifying. Perfect.

He slammed his mouth back into hers, mirroring her same need, their tongues tasting, testing, teasing. The heat of him enveloped her. He was so large it was like being surrounded by a great wall of warm stone.

"Fuck. You feel so good. Exactly like my damn dreams. I've tried to stay away. The Cape..."

He stiffened at his admission. Then slowly pulled back, shaking his head. "I'm sorry. Shit."

Dragging a hand through his hair, he sat back against the far corner of the chaise, and his hands gripped into fists at his sides.

Acute mortification swept over Larkin along with the scalding heat rising to her hairline.

"It's not you." He put his hand out, as her damn telltale blush deepened.

She shoved up from the couch. "I'm sorry. I was just trying to help. I—"

"Larkin, wait." He put out his hand but she stepped away.

What had she been thinking?

There was too much animosity between them. But he'd been in such pain; she needed to do something to ease the anguish in his eyes, even if it was just for a moment.

As she took the stairs down the front porch, her fingers flew to her lips.

He was everything she'd dreamed of, too. At least she wasn't alone in that.

But he was right. They had the Cape between them.

And no kiss in the world, no matter how earth-shattering, could change that.

CHAPTER 9

*F*riday afternoon, Ryker stared off into space at the South Cove Lobster House. He gripped the tail of his lobster in one hand and the body in the other while the taste of Larkin lingered stubbornly on his lips. Stopping her sweet seduction had been the most excruciating thing he'd ever done, but with the Cape between them, nothing good would come of letting it go further.

But, fuck. He'd really wanted to.

The feel of her skin under his hands, the scent of her filling his head, and the soft weight of her breast—

Crack!

He'd bent the tail harder than necessary for the softshell and lobster tomalley sprayed across the table, spattering Judge Carter in the face.

"Son, you act like you've never eaten a lobster before." He wiped at his chin, glaring under thick salt-and-pepper brows. "If this lunch is to win me over to your side, as I suspect, you're going at it all wrong."

"I'm sorry, sir." Ryker gripped the tail more gently in both hands and applied pressure. A softer crack sounded, then he reversed his grip and pressed it in an inside-out direction, easily separating the meat from the skeleton. He dropped it in his melted butter.

"That's more like it." The judge grumbled. "I know Maxine's taught you better, even if you have been away for a while. Once a Mainer always a Mainer."

Pulling the meat from the small bowl, Ryker shoved a large chunk into his mouth, wiping at the butter running down his chin. The soft, savory goodness was like a salve to his frustration. There was nothing better than a Maine lobster. Even those who didn't like seafood or thought it was the food of the poor—and there were plenty, regardless of what flatlanders thought—would agree.

The judge was right. He was there to turn the old guy around. He wanted to go to his investor meeting and tell them the stay was canceled and they were back in business. He just had to appeal to the judge's good-ol-boy side.

Men sticking together and all that...besides, his plan would benefit the Cape, the people, and the town. "Can't argue with you there."

Sitting on the restaurant's back deck, Ryker directed the judge's attention across the sands and open waters of the South Cove to the lighthouse, rising from the end of the Cape. Most people looked at the pristine beauty of the Cape in awe, but every time he looked, he saw all his hiding places.

"I understand your concern about me developing the Cape, sir. But my focus is on the good of the whole town."

"Well, some might argue that your plans are self-serving and downright damaging." The judge took a healthy bite of a bisquit.

"And they'd be wrong. No one bothered to ask me what my plans were in the first place. They jumped on the conservation game without doing their due diligence, and in doing so, are delaying a project that will increase town revenue." Throwing Larkin under the bus didn't feel good. In fact, he'd be hard pressed not to punch the face of anyone else who dared, but in this instance, she'd forced his hand.

"I'm listening."

"What I want is to build a community, a family of neighbors. The development would have special amenities and opportunities for the residents to thrive. As a matter of fact, the lighthouse itself will draw flatlanders in droves."

"How so?"

"I plan on renovating the lighthouse and making it available to rent for a day, a week, a month. Give flatlanders a real Maine experience. They'll wake up to the sea breeze with the morning sun and a cup from the Flat Iron Coffeehouse, then close their eyes to the stars only seen from Maine with a belly full of a North Cove Confectionery blueberry pie. The three hundred and sixty-degree view shows off the town spectacularly and will draw them in." He paused and shoved a piece of lobster in his mouth.

Swallowing, he continued, "They'll see South Cove Lobster House, hell, they can see all the way to the Fountain of Youth from there. The town itself will draw them in and guarantee a great time. And the whole experience will be directed by a concierge who specializes in our town's events."

Not to mention the cash flow would end up paying for a good portion of the Cape upkeep itself. Larkin would hate knowing she gave him the brilliant plan with her little lighthouse tour. She'd made him fall in love with the Cape, alright —in love with its ability to make him more money and get him back to New York.

Interest sparked in the judge's eyes. "I like the sound of that. Hell, now I want to stay the night. But the lighthouse itself won't provide a huge surge of commerce."

"But more than a little. And with the concierge services extending to all Cape homeowners, we'll be getting the citizens of Cape Van Buren more involved than they've ever been."

His grandmother's gentleman friend scratched his neatly groomed whiskered chin. "I like it. I like it."

"That property was meant to be lived on by families that can make happy memories there. The more families, the better the chances. And happy families mean a happy town."

"My grandson can wordsmith with the best of them, Teddy. You need to stay wicked sharp with this one." Maxine leaned in for a kiss from Ryker—and he gave her one even though she didn't deserve it—then slid in next to Carter.

Throwing her a dirty look, he shook his head. "How'd you know we'd be here?"

The judge had the courtesy to drop his eyes to the table.

"Judge Carter?" Ryker asked, but the answer was clear as the judge averted his eyes.

"Sorry, son. But when her schedule opened up, I wasn't about to miss out because we had a meeting."

"A meeting I'd have liked to hold without a spy hanging around."

Maxine scoffed. "Oh, please. So much drama."

Ryker couldn't keep his voice from rising. "You gave a character witness against me!"

"It wasn't against you so much as *for* Larkin."

With a scowl, he shoved another piece of lobster into his mouth. Though delicious, it did little to improve his mood. Right when he had the judge on his hook, his grandmother had to show up. And he wasn't about to discuss any of his other ideas with her. She'd run back and tell Larkin as soon as she had the chance.

One thing he'd learned fast in business was to never underestimate the competition. He'd recognized right away that Larkin was savvy and intelligent. She'd had the stay put in place before he'd unpacked his bags. The last thing he needed was for her to develop counter measures to offset his plans.

"Besides, you're so bent on selling the place off into pieces." She tucked a hair that was errantly blowing about in the light sea breeze behind her ear with a frustrated scowl. "You know, chopping it up into pieces and selling it off isn't going to take away any of your pain."

The lobster in his gut solidified into a ball of cement. "It'll be a good start."

"The plans I've heard so far sound pretty good, Maxine." The judge cleared his throat.

She shot him a warning look. "And what plans are those, Teddy?"

The old judge coughed into his fist and threw a pleading glance at Ryker.

"Grandma, leave him alone. And don't you dare go digging to figure out my plans. Just know I'm not destroying the Cape, I'm making it better."

She reached across the table and took his hand before he could avoid it. "I heard your dad showed up. I'm sorry. But you have to know if you destroy the Cape, if you destroy everything...your dad wins."

The sadness in her eyes killed him. She'd always felt responsible, but she wasn't. His dad had changed as an adult, and when she and Stuart had tried to get him help, he'd laughed in their faces. He was so far gone from PTSD and his alcoholism after coming back from his overseas stint in the army, he couldn't find his way back to his family.

Maxine had always told Ryker she should have found a way to help his father, but some people refused to face their demons and there was nothing that could be done. So she'd continued lavishing Ryker with love to try and make up for all the pain suffered and caused by James.

"Grammother, I'm not destroying it, and you know James isn't your responsibility." He squeezed her cool hand. With a small shake of his head, he continued. "He threatened Larkin."

That had both the judge and his grandmother leaning on the table. *"What?"*

"Before you get all riled up, she held her own. Against her better judgment if you ask me, but she gave it back better than he gave it."

Maxine beamed. "She is a scrappy thing when she gets a mind for it."

"Scrappy is one way to say it." Scrappy, sexy, smoldering...

"Ryker...Ryker." Maxine's voice broke through his musing and he shot her a look.

"Where'd you go all of a sudden?" She asked with a curious grin.

"I think the whole situation's wearing me out. That reminds me, you need to stop by and pick up all the honey. I'm assuming you've got ways to use it? Your moonshine maybe? I'm sure you've got a sale coming up."

He would have given the Cape away for a photo of the look that crossed his grandmother's face at the mention of her illegal selling of moonshine in front of the judge. He'd mat and frame that sucker.

She slapped her hand lightly to the table. "Well, I'm certain I don't know what you're talking about." Her tone was low and full of warning.

"Oh, I'm certain you do. Your moonshine is the finest kind."

Turning to face her more fully, the judge chided, "Maxine, you said you'd stopped all that business."

"Ha!" Ryker burst out. The day Maxine stopped selling her moonshine would be the day she died, God rest her soul. Grandmother wasn't one to be told what to do, and if the look on her face was any indication, the judge better mind his tongue. Ryker suspected the man was more worried about falling out of his grandmother's good graces than she was falling out of his.

Maxine narrowed her eyes at Ryker though she spoke to the judge. "You know, Teddy. It really is a shame what Ryker has planned. You know his community will destroy the beehives that Stuart nurtured with such care out at our place. Such a shame with the struggle honey bees have in this day and age."

Judge Carter nailed Ryker with a look. "Now, son, I don't like the sound of that at all. Not at all."

"But, judge, she's just trying to—"

A hand spotted with time and wrinkled with age rose and cut him off. "Son, I think we need to give Miss Sinclair time to put together her findings, then we'll rule and see who moves ahead. Yes, that's the best plan."

Ryker fell back in his seat, not bothering to hide the look of disgust on his face.

"I'll be there Sunday evening for the honey. Have dinner ready," Maxine said with a triumphant twinkle in her eye.

Well played, Maxine Van Buren. Well played. She just threw her own grandson under the bus to save her moonshine.

Though, truth be told, he didn't blame her. That shit *was* the finest kind; that was for sure.

And just now he needed a strong brew because he was back to square one with Judge Carter.

~

Sunday evening, Ryker placed the third wooden crate of jarred honey on the stack by the front door, then brushed off his hands. There would be no excuses for his grandmother to forget this way. In fact, he might just take them straight out to her car once she got here to be certain she didn't. He was still pissed at her for the little stunt she'd pulled on Friday with the judge, and the less he saw of her right now, the better.

He loved the woman, but she was enough to drive any man, woman, or child to drink.

And she'd serve up her moonshine as she did it.

The oven timer dinged and he hurried back toward the kitchen just as the doorbell rang. He yelled over his shoulder, "Come in!"

Grabbing the door handle, he peaked in then reared back as a hot waft of steam blasted him. "Shit." He pressed his fingers against his eyes, hoping he hadn't singed his damn eyelashes. "Grandmother, grab me a towel."

He put out his hand just as a soft, clean scent reached him through the savory aromas of the pizza. His grandmother wanted dinner? Fine. But something wasn't quite right.

As soon as the cloth touched his palm, he snatched it and gently dabbed at his face. "What the hell took you so long?" He blinked a few times.

It wasn't his grandmother in front of him, but Larkin, with a look of mortification on her face and miles of tanned, toned legs from a pair of shorts that had him questioning the necessity of pants.

"What are you doing here?" He didn't mean for the question to sound quite so harsh, but his brain was having a hard time rectifying the beautiful woman where his grandmother should be.

Larkin's smile was a touch timid, a tad amused, and infinitely bright. He struck the last one from the list, cursing himself for being so taken off guard. Damn women. The lot of them were nothing but trouble, though to hear them tell it, men wouldn't survive without them.

"I'm sorry, I thought you and Maxine had worked this out. She sent me to get the honey. Something about a prior engagement. Probably with Judge Carter." She shrugged.

Stepping back, Ryker smacked the side of his shin on the opened stove, then threw his hands out to either side of the stove to save himself without setting himself on fire. "God dammit," he growled, embarrassment pissing him off more than the pain did. He was fumbling around like a teenage boy with his first bra.

Cool hands caught him at the waist. "Are you okay?"

The feel of them reminded him of when she'd nursed his side after the debacle at the well and his dick decided it was the perfect moment to join the party. Fucking things should only be allowed out in very specific situations, and this wasn't one of them.

Pushing himself back from the stove, he brushed her hands from his waist, but she didn't move back. Instead, she stood just in front of him and moved her hands to his shoulders. "Are you okay? You could have really hurt yourself."

Her eyes were deep green like the leaves on the wild blueberry bushes that ran along the border of the woods. Soft fingertips trailed along his cheek, and his eyes dropped to her mouth on their own accord, leaving him hungry. He suppressed a low growl. When she looked at him like that, he wanted to sit her fine ass up on the island and ease both their frustrations.

This was going to be a problem.

Clearing his throat, he stepped back. "I'm fine. You just took me by surprise.

My grandmother said she'd be here. Though now I see she's avoiding me." Using pot holders, he removed the large pizza from the stove. "Smart woman."

"What was that?" Larkin asked.

He placed the pizza on two black spiral trivets, then leaned a hip against the counter. "Oh, nothing. Just something Maxine needs to answer to." Pulling off the pot holder mitts, he stacked one on top of the other then tossed them to the counter.

"So, she sent you to pick up the honey, did she?" he asked.

Larkin nodded. "I told her I'd be working, so I could just pick it up when I'd finished."

He ran his eyes down the length of her, admiring her luscious curves. "You're working in that?"

With a hesitant frown, she looked down at her denim shorts and blue 'eat pi' t-shirt. "What's wrong with what I'm wearing?"

Besides, the sliver of smooth skin peeking out from between her snug shirt and the waistband of her shorts that made his fingers itch to touch it, or all the leg she sported about his kitchen in bare feet as if making herself at home, not a thing. Just his damn inconvenient libido.

It was her damned fault. If she hadn't kissed him the other day, he wouldn't know just how good she tasted and want to do it again.

He waved off her question. "Nothing at all. Just concerned about injury if you're hiking about in the woods." Nodding toward the orange flip flops by the front door, he continued. "Not exactly safety first."

She rolled her eyes. "I was taking photographs along the shore today. I didn't know my attire was any of your concern."

Only when it came to his sanity.

"Find anything interesting?" The sarcastic annoyance in his voice couldn't be helped. Her presence was a constant reminder of how little control he had over his property.

Slipping her painted toes into the sandals, she nodded. But the motion was slow and a bit sad. "I did." She dipped her fingers into the front pocket of her shorts then held out a trembling hand.

A little toy army figurine lay in her palm.

His heart shifted in his chest. "Archer?"

She nodded, pulling in a shaky breath.

God. Damn. It.

He reached out and clasped her wrist. With a gentle tug, he pulled her into his arms and held her. Her small frame settled in too perfectly against his much larger body and he rested his chin on top of her head with a scowl.

All his anger rolled away in the face of her sadness. Perspective was damn inconvenient at times. But not quite as much as the heavenly feel of her in his arms, and what it made him want to do, or not do. Like let her go.

"The pizza smells good." She mumbled against his shirt.

Curse her sweet heart and silky skin.

"Do you want to stay for dinner, Cupcake?"

CHAPTER 10

What Larkin wanted was to stay wrapped up in Ryker's arms even though she had no right. The mounds of his chest cushioned her cheek and his heat warmed her soul. She couldn't remember the last time anyone had held her like this or when she'd felt as safe. Closing her eyes, she savored the moment, losing herself in his clean, masculine scent, the feel of his strong arms banding around her.

Finding Archer's toy soldier had shaken her to the core, but it also strengthened her resolve to save the Cape. She also didn't want to move out of the embrace of the one man who stood in her way.

And that would never do.

She should get the honey and go home. That had been her plan ever since Maxine tricked her into accepting the errand. The last thing she needed was to make the mistake of kissing him again. It would only make her want him more.

With a strength that surprised her, she straightened, and once his arms fell, forced herself to step away. "I'm sorry." She looked everywhere but at him.

"For what?"

She shook her head. "Archer and I were out here so often, I'm sure it won't be the last of his toys I find."

"Knowing doesn't always make it easy." His voice was like a caress of warm fingertips along her skin.

He would know more than most how little that knowledge helped in some situations. She couldn't imagine what he uncovered around every corner. The memories of his childhood held such fear and sadness for him. She pulled in a breath.

"You said something about pizza?"

He eyed the honey then nodded. "Come on. But don't let me forget to load the honey into your car. Maxine would love any excuse to come out here and harass me."

Larkin grinned behind his back as she followed him back into the quiet elegance of the kitchen. She'd go home right after dinner. "Your grandmother is an amazing woman. She's been such a dear friend to me. My parents love her."

"Everybody does. But it's different when you're her grandson. Don't get me wrong...I think Grandmother is amazing, too. But she thinks she knows what's good for me, even when I disagree. And if you know anything about Maxine, you know she doesn't stop until she's satisfied."

"That I do. After Archer died, I hid in my house for days. She didn't just knock on the door repeatedly; she broke in and doused me with a cup of water."

Ryker rounded the island with a shocked look on his face. "She did not."

Larkin giggled softly. "She did. As you can imagine, I was sputtering mad."

But then she had broken down in an anguished cry. Just like her grandson, Maxine had simply held her. It must be a Van Buren trait—comforting for comfort's sake.

He moved about the kitchen, so sure and so familiar. How didn't he see that he was home?

"She came and got me when everyone else was too afraid to upset me more." Moving to the sink, she washed her hands then turned toward the larger than life man who'd showed up in her life so unexpectedly. "What can I do to help?"

He rolled the pizza cutter through the thin crust. "There's a salad already prepared in the refrigerator. Grab it and whatever dressing you want. We can eat here." He pointed the pizza cutter toward the white marble-topped island.

She did as he asked but hesitated by the large sliding doors that led out to the back porch. "Would you be open to sitting outside? It's such a beautiful evening." She looked out across the lawn toward the South Cove. "The sky is a rainbow of colors."

"Anything you want." One side of his lips pulled into an attempt at a grin.

If only he meant it.

Grabbing white plates and black linens, he slid a hand under the pizza pan and followed her.

Once their fare was set up on the black slate of the outdoor table, Larkin lightly slapped her leg. "Crap."

His eyes lingered on her thighs and she could feel the heat rising along her skin.

"What?" He dragged his eyes up her body until they met hers. It seemed like an effort, which made her feel more beautiful than she had in a long time. Maybe all the excitement and activity lately was doing her some good after all.

"I forgot my hoody in the car. I'll go grab it."

Ryker pulled out her chair. "I'll grab you one from inside. Just give me a second."

He returned with two sweatshirts. One he handed to her and the other he pulled over his head.

She hesitated as the scent of his cologne weaved its magic about her head.

"Will that work? I figured I'd save you the trip."

"What?" She startled. "Yes, of course." She shoved her arms through and pulled the sweatshirt over her head.

His laugh met her ears as she tugged it into place. The hem of it fell past her shorts.

"You could wear that thing as a dress. And with those legs..." He added, with a curious edge to his voice. He stood close and his fingers brushed along the edge of the sweatshirt against the sensitive skin of her thigh, sending a wash of goosebumps along her skin and leaving a tight ball of sensation at her center.

Her eyes flew to his and he stepped back, coughing into his hand and gesturing to the pizza. "Let's eat before the breeze cools it down too much."

She swore the look in his eyes alone would warm her for a lifetime, but she was thankful for the sweatshirt now that the sun was setting, and she sat down. "But that's the magic of pizza. It's always good."

They dug into their dinner in silence. Ryker stopped eating long enough to light the fireplace flanking the long table, and the warmth was just right, like the stars in the sky and the sound of the waves cresting then crashing against the shore.

Like the man sitting so close yet so far across the table.

"I need you to understand something. But I don't want to hurt you by bringing it up." His deep voice washed over her.

She wiped her mouth with her napkin then gripped it on her lap. His tone was serious and left a buzz of nervous anticipation in her chest—not the excited kind but the heavier, scared kind. Something to focus on while they chatted would help. Anything to give her a little distance. "Okay. This sounds big. But can we pick some blueberries while we chat? I'd love to make a pie later."

Ryker tilted his head. "I didn't mean to come across so somberly. It's not that big of a deal, though I know talking about Archer must be hard on you. But yeah, let's pick some blueberries. Though they budded early this year, they're not going to be ripe."

"I know. I want tart more than sweet."

The sun was dipping past the trees west of the Cape, leaving the grounds more shaded than the time of day called for, but the white-capped blue of the berries could still be seen along the low bushes spreading out like a lake along the southern border of the Cape by the trees.

The back porch had a long work area and lower storage bins held baskets of every variety as well as gloves and small hand tools. The larger yard tools were stored in a shed that shared the same dark, elegant colors as the house.

Peering inside the lower cabinet, he called out. "How big of a basket do you want?"

She stepped up behind him to look over his shoulder just as he stood with a basket in his hand. Their chests brushed against each other and a spark of pleasure rushed across her breasts.

He reached out to steady her with hands she kept dreaming about. "We seem to be doing a lot of this lately."

A small, shaky laugh floated off on the breeze as she took the basket from his hand. She couldn't figure out her reaction to him. The pull to be close but the need to stay away.

She held up the basket. "This will do just fine."

They stepped carefully into the spread of lowbush blueberries with miles of silence between them, the sounds of their steps barely audible over the crashing waves along the shores and the songbirds in the trees.

As she bent to look over a few bushes, he cleared his throat. "When you found Archer's toy. What did that make you feel?"

She paused with a few blueberries in her hand. They weren't quite as vibrant as they would be in a few weeks, a bit more purple than blue.

"It stole my breath." She answered softly, then popped a berry in her mouth, thankful for the overly tart zing needed to ground her. "It rushed me back through time to the last moment he'd played with the toy. I could hear his sweet laugh, see the happy light in his eyes. His blond hair ruffled from the ocean breeze."

Her chest ached as the memory hit her once more.

"It was both beautiful and torturous. It reminds me of what I no longer have. Will never have again." She blinked rapidly, willing her throat to open so she could swallow the blueberry. "But it also reminded me of my perfect love."

She handed him the basket, noting the sadness in his gaze and appreciating the compassion. He might seem like an ass when it came to the Cape, but he had a heart, and it hurt for her. "Hold this for me." Then one by one, she chose which berries to add to it. Almost ripe, but not quite, they'd make the perfect compote for her pie. Archer had loved her pies. She pulled in a shaky breath.

Ryker's voice joined the sounds of the settling day.

"When I walk through this land, all I see are my hiding places. The large, hollowed out stump of a dying tree, the overhang of stone along the north shore, even the lighthouse, though that proved to be a mistake."

She listened while she made her choices, dropping her berries into the basket. Her hand brushed against his and his eyes found hers.

They were full of anguish. "The memories steal my breath, too, and the sensation I'm left with is fear, the sounds I hear are my mother crying out or me grunting as my father's fists hit home. I tried my hardest to keep quiet because my screams only egged him on."

Her stomach soured and she rose to stand in front of him. "Ryker."

His brows were drawn together, giving his dark looks an edge that made her tremble.

"I'm not telling you this for your sympathy—I'm telling you to help you understand where I'm coming from. Why I have to do this. And why I'm asking you to reconsider."

She took the basket of berries from him, hoping to ease his burden. "I can't imagine. Really, I can't. But don't you see? You're focusing on the wrong thing." Her chest tightened, wanting to get through to him, to help him.

"Aren't you listening?" He swung away from her then back. "It hurts me to be here. And you want me to change my focus?" His words came out just shy of a frustrated shout, but she held her ground.

"Yes." She pleaded. "If you could remember back to good memories of your grandmother, working the bees with your grandfather. What memories here make you feel something other than fear? Focus on that." She forced her words out, willing him to concentrate on what could give him peace instead of what was clearly his hell.

He stepped in front of her, so big and tall, he blocked out the moon that was now casting a soft glow on the white-capped blueberries. "You want me to focus on what makes me feel good?"

"Yes." Finally. She was getting through to him.

Something shifted in his eyes, something intense and dangerous and unknown. "Fine." He growled so softly she barely heard him.

His arms swept around her body, pulling her in, crushing her against his unyielding chest. The basket of berries dropped to the ground. A thrill of sensation shot through her body at the contact, but before she could respond, his mouth was on hers, obliterating the light from the moon. Her world went black in a spiraling wave of sensation with the feel of his lips and the stroke of his tongue.

He held her with one hand, while he dragged the other over her hip, then up her side, past her breast, until he cupped her cheek. Angling her head to suit his needs, he dove even deeper, taking her with him.

She grabbed handfuls of his hair, not sure how they got there in the first place but needing a solid hold on something before she lost her footing. Without warning, the hand wrapped around her back dropped low and he lifted her against his chest until she wrapped her legs around his waist.

The heat of his body scorched her legs, and the hard length of him pressed home against her center, sending mini-pulses of pleasure through her body. His hand slid from her face into her hair, and he gripped hard.

He was unrelenting and her body rejoiced in each grab, caress, and slide of his hands against her. For so long, she'd been living a dormant life. A shell of who she used to be. But since meeting Ryker, she felt alive. Part of that was the urgency to save the Cape, to do something good in memory of her son, but another part of it was this giant of a man holding her as if she were nothing more than a feather.

She'd tried to resist the soft heart he'd shown toward Maxine, the kindness in working with his bees, the haunted look in his eyes when he remembered the scared little boy he used to be. But each day, each moment with him was making it more difficult.

Three steps took them out of the lowbush and onto the soft grass. He lowered her to the ground, following right along until the weight of him pressed home. She let out a ragged groan, reveling in the feel of his body between her legs and his hands on her breasts.

Trailing kisses along her jaw, he suckled her earlobe, then moved on to the sensitive skin along the side of her neck.

"Fuck. You feel...so damn good," he rasped out on a groan.

He settled his hand on her thigh then slowly trailed up, the rough calluses of his fingers causing goose bumps to scatter across her skin and proving he was much more than a paper pusher. With her leg drawn up, he continued his journey, cupping her exposed cheek from the hem of her shorts. His fingers slid around the globe, making her suck in a breath every time they traveled close to her center.

His mouth found hers once again just as the tips of his fingers struck home in a light, slick stroke.

She reared up against his hip. "Oh God."

"You're so wet for me, Larkin. Do you feel that?"

He continued stroking her, sliding his fingers along her folds, then dipping just the tip of two inside.

"Ryker!"

Teasing his tongue along hers, he tasted, savored, then sucked in her lower lip, never once slowing his light strokes against her flesh.

Her body tightened with a familiar, coiling need that she vaguely remembered and at the same time had never known. One hand gripped his shirt and the other tufts of grass, trying to find stability. Trying to keep from falling.

"Come for me, Larkin. Give me something good to hold on to in this place." His whisper was ragged against her ear as he grazed his teeth along her lobe.

She wrapped her arms around his neck and poured herself into kissing him with every ounce of passion she experienced beneath his fingertips. "I'm here."

Her body trembled and strained against his hand as her desire peaked and waves of intense pleasure crashed over her body. She pressed her lips against the rapid pulse in his neck, silencing her scream until she could breathe once again.

"Christ, woman."

She dragged her lips against his neck to the stubble on his chin, finding his delicious mouth once again. He was the ocean and the whole night sky all wrapped in one overwhelming man.

As her body settled and breathing calmed, her brain cleared. His words registered with a crash back to reality. A reality that included her falling in love with a man she had no right to even care about.

She kept her arms wrapped tightly around him, afraid of what it meant when she let him go.

All he wanted to invest in was the future when she found true value in the past. Why the hell her heart didn't understand that was beyond her.

She couldn't be what made him feel good on the Cape because no matter how painful his past was to him; her past was where she found her joy.

His kiss had brought her to life, but saving the Cape would keep her living.

CHAPTER 11

*S*he ran.

It didn't matter how many days went by or how Ryker went over it in his head; the result was the same. Larkin had run.

And it cut deep.

Not only had she taken off after what was the hottest make-out sessions he'd ever had, but she'd also left a damned thank you note and preserves from Janice's garden on his doorstep sometime Monday afternoon.

Her little drop-and-dashes were becoming a habit.

Coward.

He grumbled under his breath as he hauled a bucket of salt water from the North Cove waters onto the bow of the sailboat deck. His grandfather's boat had been docked for the past year without any upkeep, and since he could do little about the stay on his property—for the moment—he could do something about the sorry state of the teak deck.

A good scrubbing would let him see how many teak plugs had popped out and what condition the compound was in between the planks. Maxine had started cutting back and trimming down on maintenance of the property before Ryker had even signed the dotted line, and it showed.

He scowled, grabbing the bucket and pouring a bit of the salt water onto the decking. The gray, dirty wood gave him a good outlet for his restlessness.

Surely the way he'd been feeling since Sunday had everything to do with the progress he wasn't making with his project and not the hot, raw need he experienced every time he was around Larkin or the fact she'd practically run to her car after their little excursion in the blueberry bushes.

Grabbing a stiff brush, he scrubbed back and forth over the teak. He worked on one section at a time, adding salt water then scrubbing, again and again. His shoulders burned and his back ached but it was better than the tight urgency to call Larkin.

When they'd gone out to pick blueberries, his heart warred with the pain on her face as she spoke about the loss of Archer and the punch of desire in his gut as she'd bent over in those damn shorter-than-should-be-legal shorts.

But he'd held it together until she'd pushed him, until she demanded that he focus on what made him feel good on the Cape.

Her responsive body under him had sure as shit felt amazing.

But her running away had not.

Once again, he didn't measure up in some way that he wasn't meant to understand. Like why his grandfather didn't leave him the Cape and what had made James beat him in the first place.

Fuck. He hated the feeling of inadequacy. He was a goddamn successful businessman who had conquered the most challenging city in the United States.

This was why he should have never come back here. Why he had to separate from the Cape once and for all.

Shaking his head, he attacked the teak with vigor. The burn in his arms would make him forget everything else.

Like the honey still sitting by his damn front door. For the past two days, every time he passed it he'd think of how Larkin had tasted, the silky slide of her skin, and had to fight the urge to take it to her so they could do it all over again.

It was more than her fragile beauty. He couldn't stop thinking about the stubborn lift in her chin when he challenged her, the passionate spark in her eyes when she taught him about a rare butterfly, or the way she pulled her shoulders back instead of crumpling to the ground like he imagined she'd rather do when speaking of her son.

He slammed the brush back into the bucket, splashing water in a wide arc.

"Whoa. What the hell's wrong with you?" Mitch jumped back, though his deck shoes still took a hit.

Ryker kept scrubbing. "How'd you know I was out here?"

"It's Cape Van Buren. News travels fast when the town hermit ventures away from his cave."

"How the hell am I the town hermit? No one even knows me here anymore."

Mitch rested a hand atop a stanchion. "Exactly. Name one time you've been downtown since arriving? It's going to be mighty hard to convince the judge you have Cape Van Buren's best interest at heart when you won't even go to town."

"Goddamnit." Ryker tossed the brush to the deck then grabbed the bucket and rinsed the area he'd scrubbed.

"Did you hear what the hell Maxine did to me with the judge last week?"

Mitch started laughing, making Ryker want to punch the humor from the dick's face.

Raising his hands, his buddy rolled his eyes. "Get that look off your face. You have to admit, your grandmother's brilliant. My mom and Evette were howling about it over some blueberry and poppy moonshine." He smacked his lips. "Damn fine."

"Great. Glad you're all having a fucking ball. It's all fun and games until my investors back out and you're out of a job."

Mitch cleared his throat. "Yeah, about that..."

A heavy weight settled in Ryker's gut. If they pulled out, he'd be screwed. Van Buren Enterprises had already sunk a shit ton of money into surveying the project and acquiring licenses up front. "What now?"

"They want to meet at the end of the week. And we better have some good news."

Ryker wiped his brow with the back of his hand. The summer sun chose today to be relentless and scrubbing the deck wasn't helping. Grabbing the hem of his t-shirt, he pulled it over his head then threw it on top of the forward hatch.

"This day's just getting better and better."

Mitch stared past Ryker's shoulder. "It's certainly looking up from where I'm standing."

Ryker turned to find Larkin walking up the dock toward the boat. The bottom of her sundress played peek-a-boo with her thighs in the wind, and she had on the same flip flops from her last visit to the Cape. Why the hell he'd noticed that was beyond him. He raked his hand through his hair.

There was more color in her face since he'd first met her, a bit of a glow that hadn't been there before. She smiled, then her eyes fell on him and she stutter-stepped a bit. Suddenly, eye contact seemed impossible and the smile on her lips appeared strained.

He glanced down at his bare chest, then back to her. Good. He was glad it made her nervous. Payback for his immediate hard-on and the twisted feeling in his gut.

She focused on Mitch as she stepped aboard. "Hello there, gentlemen."

Mitch stepped forward in all his golden boy glory and took her hand.

"Thank you," she said.

His buddy rubbed a fist over his heart, holding her gaze with a look Ryker wouldn't trust if his life depended on it. "My pleasure."

Yeah. Yeah. Move over, Casanova.

Ryker stepped between them, forcing Mitch back to his original position.

Larkin held his gaze with a hard swallow. "Hey."

He nodded once. "What are you doing here?"

Her eyes scanned over his features, leaving him to feel more naked than if he'd taken off his pants instead of his shirt. "I thought I'd check with you about that honey for Maxine."

He crossed his arms over his chest, restraining his smile as her eyes dropped to his biceps. It soothed his soul somewhat to see a familiar need there. "Have you considered my question?"

Green eyes flared wide. "Question?"

"About the Cape. Our discussion. The chance of you reconsidering."

A look of comprehension relaxed the crease in her brow and a hint of something he remembered as hope settled home in his chest.

But then she shook her head. "I thought we were just talking. Sharing. I didn't think you were serious."

"Why wouldn't I be serious?" He couldn't help that his voice was rising. He'd never felt as misunderstood as he did back in his hometown.

Mitch stepped forward. "Ryker."

Placing a hand to his forearm, she licked her lips then glanced over to Mitch and back. "I thought you understood. I have to do this."

The sensation from her hand on his skin fanned out as quickly as his hope died. He stepped away. Deep down, he wanted to yell and cuss and demand she get the hell off his boat, but one thing life in New York had taught him was how to keep a level head. How to remain logical, unattached, and devoid of emotion when it came to business.

He dipped his chin. "The honey is where we left it. Door's open."

Squatting back down to the deck, he grabbed the brush in a tight grip.

She hesitated, the smile on her face wavering with what looked like hurt. Giving a small wave to Mitch, she made her way back off his boat. Away from him. Again.

Having her around tied him in knots but watching her leave tore him in two. He was wicked fucked.

Shoving his thoughts away with ruthless determination, he ignored Mitch and focused on the deck.

If she wouldn't reconsider, then he'd simply find a way to make sure he was awarded the rights to his property. He had to step up his game. Uncover the judge's weak point, what appealed to him and the town. Ryker wasn't successful in business because of his good looks.

He was fearless and tireless, and it was time to bring those traits to the Cape.

~

The North Cove Mavens and their honorary sidekicks bent their heads together to look at the plan Janice had drawn up. Larkin nudged Blayne until she moved over and gave her a little more room as Maxine pointed to a bush sculpture of a peacock with its feathers decked out in different colored pansies.

"Those South Cove Madams won't know what hit them when they get a load of this," she said.

Larkin reached up and tucked the chic silver hair behind Maxine's ear to reveal her face and looked her in the eye. "But we can't underestimate them. We have creativity on our side but they have logic on theirs."

"Harrumph!" Evette crossed her bony arms across her chest. Her dark hair was pulled back in a severe ponytail and she was sporting deep red lips that rivaled Blayne's. "They may be logical but we see in color."

Blayne nodded her head. "Agreed. But they are really good at keeping their emotions in check and their moves deliberate."

Janice threw her arms up in the air, her red curls bouncing. "Deliberate? Deliberate? You don't call this deliberate?"

"Mom, where can I set these?" Mitch Brennan walked up with four bags of potting soil loaded in his arms. His blond hair glinted in the sun as did his biceps in the heavy summer heat.

Blayne cleared her throat. Mitch looked at Larkin in surprise. "Hey there, Ms. Sinclair."

"Are you kidding me with that right now? I just saw you."

He glanced around, shifting from one foot to the other. Why the hell he'd be nervous made no sense to her at all, but she had enough to worry about with Ryker.

Turning to his mother, he asked. "Mom?"

Janice waved him toward the garden's edge. "Over there. Thanks, sweetie."

Evette, Maxine, Larkin, and Blayne watched as he made his way across the lawn. His muscles bounced and bulged in a way that any woman with a pulse could appreciate.

Janice chuckled. "Anyway, ladies. We're creating an ostentation of peacocks, a bird that stands for integrity and beauty. Exactly what you'll find in the Mavens."

That snapped them out of Mitch's man-muscle spell.

"Not to mention, nobility and holiness," Evette added with a rapid nod.

Larkin watched her friends out of the corner of her eyes, overcome by the rush of love that helped warm the cold hollow space in her chest that was a constant companion. She pointed at the arm flapping and vigorous nodding between Janice and Evette. "Yeah. This is what I'm talking about. You Mavens are a passionate lot. Which is not a bad thing, but—"

Maxine grinned. "You Mavens? Please, you talk like you aren't from the north side. But you got that right. I'll have you know Teddy is quite the master in—

Larkin and Blayne covered their ears, chanting, "La la la la la!" The last thing they wanted to hear was anything concerning Maxine's sex life with the Judge. Besides, it was a bit demoralizing that her friend had more sex these days than she did.

To her credit, up until two days ago, it had been over two years since she'd been touched in general but a lifetime of ever being touched the way Ryker had touched her.

Those hands. Holy shit. A shiver shook her shoulders.

She still couldn't believe she'd run away.

How.

Mortifying.

It had all come down to self-preservation and a need to stay focused on the Cape. Something he made increasingly difficult with his appealing dark gaze and that kissable mouth. The thought of his taste sent a spiral of sensations through her body and deposited them on her lips. Both pairs.

She pressed her mouth into a tight line to ease the tingling reminder.

But she was a big girl and had promised Maxine to get the honey.

And then forgot.

So she'd faced him today at the marina.

In all his dark and bronze glory. There was no doubt his shoulders were wide, but to see them stretched out over his chest while he was working...his very well formed, very well filled out, mounds of muscled—

"Larkin!" All four ladies shouted.

"What?!" She shouted back with a jump.

Blayne laughed. "I don't know where you just disappeared to, but wherever it was, you liked it." She pointed to the deep red flush over Larkin's chest and neck.

Ignoring her friends, she looked over the garden plan for the festival. They only had four days left to create their wonderland of botanical masterpieces and rumor had it the South Cove Madams were pulling out all the stops this year.

She grabbed a small green, plastic tube, added a smidge of flower food, then topped it off with water. Settling on a grouping of purple pansies, she removed a couple with their roots intact and slid them through the cross-slit of a rubber lid. With the lid snapped into place, she studied it with a critical eye. Every individual flower cluster they created would be used to represent the colors in a peacock's feather. And, thanks to Janice, they had every color under the sun—if they could keep Maxine from stealing them for her moonshine.

"It really will be beautiful, but may I make a suggestion?" Larkin asked, hesitant to get any of them excited again. Her nerves couldn't take it.

She set her pansies in a large bowl with the flowers sticking over the rim. "What if we use blue glass stepping stones as kind of a river that flows through the garden? Guests walk through the garden instead of just around it. We can have little stations that give information about peacocks, their meaning, and the flowers. Make it interactive."

"I have beautiful peacock note cards we can use for the information cards. All I'd need to do is laminate them," Blayne offered.

Maxine stared at the two women with a hard look. Then her eyes lit up and she grabbed Janice by the arm. "This is brilliant." She looked to Evette.

All the ladies nodded.

"But do you think we can finish it in time? We only have three days left," Blayne reminded them.

Larkin counted off on her fingers what they'd need to get done, not to mention her continued work out on the Cape. "It's going to be tough but—"

Claire Adams rounded the corner by the North Cove Condos at the south end of the garden.

"We'd be able to do it if we had one more pair of hands." Larkin pointed across the garden.

All four women shook their heads.

"You're mad." Blayne cut through the air with her palm. "You've just now come out from under your widow's rock. Having to see Claire all the time will just push you right back under."

"No. It won't," Larkin insisted. "She needs this. I've had all of you. Who has she had?" She needed someone, something, and Larkin was determined to give it to her.

Maxine glanced at the woman. "But she's South Cove; no way are we letting her in. That'd be like inviting Teddy over while I'm selling my moonshine." She shuddered.

Larkin's jaw dropped open. "Maxine. You know as well as I do that she's never done anything with the South Cove Madams. She's a loner. Besides, we already established they aren't the most nurturing bunch. If anyone's tried to help her at all, it's probably been with a slap to her back and a 'you got this!' cheer."

"What is this really about?" Blayne asked, worry shining from her green eyes.

"I just..." Watching Claire walk toward them, she shook her head. "I've got to help her. I had you, and it still took two years to get me moving past simply existing. And I've only just started."

Janice added the prepared pansies to the bowl, making a beautiful hemisphere of color. "Let's do it." She pushed her curls from her face. "We have too much to do to be picky now. Besides, with the wicked awesome idea you two girls had, there's no way South Cove will win even if they had a year to copy our plan."

Larkin slapped her hands together on a grin. "Come help me."

"I am not—

"Blayne." She gave her best friend a hard stare.

She rolled her eyes. "Fine. But if I see one iota of evidence that this is hurting you, I'm ending it."

"Fine." Larkin slid her arm through Blayne's.

With her stomach twisting into a knot, Larkin forced her gaze to stay relaxed but direct. "Hello, Claire."

The young woman snapped her head up then let out a sigh. "Why are you everywhere these days?"

Pasting a smile on her lips, Larkin released Blayne and fell into step next to Claire. At least the two of them were no longer crying every time they saw each other.

The woman looked her up and down with suspicion. "What...do you want?" The tone in her voice was both pleading and exasperated.

"We need your help. And before you say no..."

"Smart woman. At least I'll give you that."

Larkin resisted the urge to grit her teeth. "The North Cove Mavens need an extra pair of hands to complete our garden design by Friday."

"No." Claire tried to step away.

"There's a bottle of free moonshine with your name on it if you do."

That had her stopping in her tracks. "Mrs. Van Buren's moonshine?"

Larkin had trouble wrapping her mind around the Mrs. Van Buren title. Maxine was such a feisty every-girl's kind of woman who always laughed off any mention of status. If she heard Claire call her that, no amount of begging would get her to hand over a bottle of her moonshine. For any price.

"Yeah, but let's call her Maxine. She gets a bit snappy with the 'Mrs.' kind of thing."

Blayne yawned. "You don't have to join us. I keep telling them we'll finish in plenty of time.

Larkin sent her a raised brow.

Claire lifted her chin. "Fine. If I get the bottle of moonshine, I'm in." She eyed Larkin warily. "This is going to mean I have to chat with you, won't it?"

Larkin would have grinned, but the glassy look in the young woman's eye warned of tears, not good humor. "I'm hoping," she said softly.

"Are you in or not? We haven't got all day." Blayne slid her arm back through Larkin's, always a mama bear before a pussy cat.

Claire shot Blayne a hard stare, then the corners of her mouth trembled into a small grin. "I like you. Your annoyance is a hell of a lot better than the pity I get from everyone else."

Larkin reached for her. "I'm sure they're all just—"

Claire raised a hand. "Stop while you're ahead. Make sure you don't forget the moonshine. I've been wanting to try that for years but never had the right connections. Except for Mitch Brennan, but he's no different now than when we were kids. Annoying with a side of irritation, but in a much bigger body."

Larkin and Blayne exchanged knowing glances, reading between the lines of Claire's griping.

"I'll run home and change and head on over to the gardens." Claire took off without looking back.

Blayne pulled Larkin back toward the Mavens. "So a bottle of moonshine, huh? How are you going to swing that? Maxine doesn't sell to strangers. She loves you like a daughter and barely comes off one for you."

That *was* going to be a problem but she had to figure out a plan. The urgency to pull Claire into the fold, to help her like Larkin's friends had grew stronger with each passing day that she worked to save the Cape. Somehow the two missions had melded into one.

A few ideas popped into Larkin's head, but they all included intense dark eyes and a mouth that inspired fantasies. She needed to steer clear of that man.

But he might be the only one who could get her that moonshine.

CHAPTER 12

*W*ednesday afternoon, Larkin stepped through the fresh cut grass, focusing on the silky blades as they slid over her toes. This part of the lawn was crisp and groomed and emerald. It served as a wonderful contrast to the exciting untamed and natural areas of the Cape that ran the perimeter. Rough rocky shores, tall blue joint grasses, and the rare blue leaf willow trailed along the edge of the shore above the rocks.

It made her think of Ryker. He too was both well-groomed and ruggedly sexy.

Which she didn't need to think about. Especially now.

He was the reason she was on the Cape to work instead of play in the first place.

Stepping up to the well, the familiar squeeze of sadness constricted her chest. Two weeks had already passed since Archer's birthday, since the beginning of her mission to save his Cape. The days without him kept slipping by while the years that stretched out before her seemed endlessly long.

But the only time that mattered now was the less than two weeks she had left to propose her findings and save the Cape.

Time to focus and stay determined.

Just as she had to do with Claire yesterday. She'd talked her into helping the Mavens, but spending time with the woman turned out to be just what Blayne had warned her it would be. The Cape reminded her of Archer when he was alive, running through the tall grasses with Puzzle, his laughter carrying on the wind. But seeing Claire reminded her of his death.

Of the mangled car.

Of no turning back. Or moving forward.

It was as though she were stuck in the horrible moment when she'd learned he'd died. Nothing would ever be the same, and every day after was excruciating.

Pulling in a shaky breath, she ran her fingers over her locket, relieved by the weight of it in her hand and against her heart.

She walked around the well, counting through the flowers planted at the base. They'd grown since Ryker had saved her necklace. She studied the flowers where he'd hung himself over the edge, his and her feet digging in to keep him top side.

Peering closer at the flowers, a small smile pulled at the corners of her lips.

Though crushed that day, they'd bounced back. They stood tall, a few petals bruised but otherwise blooming.

Now that was determination.

"Okay, Archer," she whispered. "I hear you."

Dropping her locket back to her chest, she reached for the damaged but thriving blooms. They were silky under her fingertips.

So fragile.

Yet here they were.

And so was she. It was time to make it count.

Choosing a hardy flower that hadn't been fighting to recover, she plucked the stem low to the ground then tucked it behind her ear. When she got home, she'd press it between the pages of her favorite book. A reminder of how strong she could be.

Glancing up and down the length of the Cape, she checked the time. Ryker was in town or so the gossips that were her crazy friends had informed her this morning while they worked with their peacocks in the garden.

She didn't mean to hide but clarity and focus were not easily maintained with him around.

Her heart was wrapping around someone who would never want the encumbrance. Not to mention she struggled with every story she heard about his childhood. In any other situation, she'd help him in any way she could to heal from his heartache. But she just couldn't this time. Healing his past, his way, meant destroying hers.

And she would always be stuck.

With one last look at the flowers around the well, she pulled out her phone. Swiping through her screens, she pulled up her notes then snapped a few photos.

She took pictures and measurements of the blue joint, then slowed down to really study the blue leaf willow. It was rare inland but in abundance on the Cape. Pulling a small waxed paper envelope from her bag, she removed a leaf section, then slid it inside. A little closer look at her office at work would let her determine the overall health of the plant.

Along with the crowberry blue butterfly and the Yellow Spotted Salamander, she was building quite the argument for conserving the Cape. Not to mention the bees. And if she was right, there was an Italian honey bee hive pretty close to a Carniolan bee hive. If they weren't cared for properly, the Italians would steal from the others, which also risked spreading disease and destroying the hive.

She made her way down the familiar path into the woods. As soon as she stepped within the grouping of trees, the world was blanketed from all the noise of life. It was much darker inside and an ethereal glow illuminated the space with sunlight filtered through so many leaves.

Keeping her distance, she located the hive and tried to get a closer look. The honey bees might be her Hail Mary for saving the Cape. But she was hoping not to need one. Her recommendation was solid. The board just had to care.

She frowned.

The soft hum of the little suckers met her ears. There was no way in hell she was going any closer. The threat of never tasting Maxine's moonshine ever again wouldn't even budge her.

Up on tiptoes, she squinted but still couldn't identify which bees the hive had.

Damn it.

"What're you doing, Cupcake?"

The question came from behind her and she spun around so fast she almost fell.

Ryker reached out to help her but she threw her hands out to ward off any assistance. Seeing his dark gaze hooded by strong brows and supported by a twisted grin was bad enough. If he touched her, she feared she'd succumb to her overwrought, long-denied hormones and ease her frustrations by tackling him to the ground.

"I'm okay. I got it." She pushed her hair out of her face. "I scared you."

He raised a brow. "What?"

Heat crawled up her neck. "I mean, you scared me." *Good God, woman. Pull yourself together.*

Approaching slowly, his gaze slid over her from head to toe. Her sundress suddenly felt too tight and her light rain jacket, which she wore to ward off the cooling evening temperatures, now seemed sweltering. Ignoring him, she peered back at the hive. "What kind of bees are those?"

"I thought you hated bees."

"I told you, I don't hate them." She stepped toward the bench, watching out for the salamander she'd found last time. Peaking at him, she worked hard at shoving down the waves of awareness from his proximity.

Then she saw the hummingbird feeders, each of them filled with nectar, and her heart turned over. She trailed a finger along the edge of one red feeder.

"You filled them." She gestured toward the tiny birds.

He dipped his chin then turned back to the beehive with a content look on his face. Must be nice to feel that way. It only confused her more that he could let it all go.

"I thought you were in town." She bit the inside of her lip. The last thing she meant to do was admit she'd been keeping tabs.

"Why are you avoiding me?" His tone was low but direct.

She half laughed. "I'm not, I..." Staring at her coral-painted toes, she ran through possible excuses but came up short. A shadow fell over the ground she was hoping would swallow her whole.

"Larkin."

Please don't touch me. Please don't touch me. She repeated the wish over and over in her head as his hand reached for her.

Warm fingers slid along her cheek and she grabbed them. "I can't do this. It's too complicated."

"No, it's not. It just is what it is." He stepped closer.

She put her hand on his chest. "Wait." In a quick move, she skirted around him. "I think you have different subspecies of bees here on the Cape."

She glanced back to find him watching her with a curious expression.

He walked toward her, and her mind tried to argue but her body hummed with an awareness that told her his interest was way more biological than environmental.

"Anyway," she continued warily as he got closer. "If you have Italian bees, you're at risk of losing whole hives. They like to steal and they aren't nice about it." With a quick look back to the hive, she pulled in a nervous breath. "In fact, you may have already."

He stood in front of her, overwhelming, encompassing. "I know."

She stared dumbly. "Oh."

"I'm going to kiss you now, Larkin." He slid his hands up her arms to her shoulders.

"But why? You know this is a bad idea."

He held her gaze with one corner of his lips kicked up in a half grin. "I've told myself that at least million times. But here I am. Drawn to you. Whether I like it or not."

"I don't like it either."

On a chuckle, he stepped closer. "Then we have that in common. There's no pressure..." He slid his fingers from her shoulders up along the sensitive skin of her neck in a slow circular motion. "...no expectations. This doesn't have to go anywhere. I know you're not ready for anything serious."

She stared at his mouth, swearing she could feel it on her even though he hadn't kissed her yet. And since when wasn't she interested in anything serious? No one'd ever asked her if she was. Hell, she hadn't asked herself. It certainly wasn't any hang up on John. The thought of him left her numb, little more than a layer of guilt for not feeling more. They'd been drifting apart years ago, and after what he did...

The combination of the soft skin of Ryker's fingertips with the calluses along the ridge of his palm sent a shiver down her spine.

What did she want?

The Cape.

But for her future? For love?

Biting on the inside of her lip, she studied this man who clouded her brain and set her body aflame. She wanted a future on the Cape—she wanted love. She wanted to do more than dream of feeling alive; she wanted to really feel it. And if she crashed and burned afterward then so be it.

She had to quit hiding behind her grief.

Swallowing hard as his hand moved up to gently cup her cheek, she tilted her head into his warmth.

He plucked the flower from her ear. "What's this?" His whisper held a husky edge to it.

Proof that even something fragile could survive and thrive. But she couldn't say that. Not to him. Not now.

If she wanted to live, it was time to live. And on her terms.

Whether it was the romantic glow of this magical place with fireflies flickering on and off like nature's own string of lights, or the low humming music from the bees, or pure, simple loneliness, she wasn't sure. But she wanted to feel something beyond the hollow space left in her chest. She wanted to feel...him.

Sucking in a breath, she slipped her arms around his neck and pressed against his chest. His arms immediately banded about her waist, lifting her higher. She slid her lips over his lower one then tasted his top one before diving deeper still.

A low rumbling groan reverberated from his chest to hers and he whispered against her mouth, "Fuuuuuck."

"My thoughts exactly." She kissed him harder, trying to ease the rising urgency she'd felt since meeting him.

She slowly broke the kiss, resting her forehead against his. "But here? I don't have any..." Her voice was barely above a whisper.

His mouth stretched wide and he dug deep in his back pocket. The glint of foil sparkled in the low light. He looked around them.

"Here is perfect. Our very own secluded haven."

In the waning light, they transcended into a secret fairyland where, just maybe, everything she'd ever dreamed might come true. The air was humid but light. As evening drew closer, the temperature dropped while her own skin burned.

She shrugged out of her jacket, tossing it to the bench. Swallowing hard, she slid her thumbs under the thin straps of her dress and peeked at Ryker.

The intensity in his dark eyes left her trembling. Was she crazy to want this?

With his jaw clenched, he placed his hands over hers.

"Let me," he rasped out.

Heat flushed up her neck at his touch and he chuckled softly, following the trail of red with his tongue.

"Ryker?"

"Hmmm?" Pulling each strap over her shoulders, he let the dress continue to hang as he trailed his tongue and lips along the sensitive skin of her neck and jaw. Finally reaching her mouth, he pulled her in, and she wanted to savor the feel of him pressing against her aching breasts.

"I don't know if I remember how to do this." Her whisper joined the hum of the woods.

He immediately stopped and held her gaze. Drawing one finger over her brows then down the bridge of her nose, he said, "We don't have to do this. Just don't avoid me. Life is full of hard things, but that's what makes you feel alive."

She stared back, afraid to move forward but more afraid to step back. It would never work between them, but this moment... This moment was her chance to live, maybe even love.

"I want this. I'm just..."

"Scared? Hell, woman. You terrify me."

She chuckled at the thought. It was ridiculous to think anything could ever scare this hulk of man. "I do not."

Sliding both hands up to softly cup her face, he said, "More than anything. In fact, I have a feeling you might destroy me." His voice was low and as dark as his words.

Larkin blinked, immediately wanting to deny it, but the hard truth was he might be right. But she still couldn't stop fighting to save her memories. She couldn't stop fighting against his goals. And she could stop fighting against the irresistible pull to taste him and feel him and wrap herself in his masculine scent.

Dropping unsteady hands to his waist, she shoved aside his shirt then unbuttoned his jeans. Every time her trembling fingers slid against his hard abs, he sucked in a breath. He ran his big, warm hands over her shoulders, giving the straps of her dress a tug. In one *swoosh*, the dress fell to the ground, leaving her in nothing but a nude pair of panties.

He took in the sight of her peaked nipples with hungry eyes. "You are stunning."

His words emboldened her and she grabbed the hem of his shirt, lifting it up and over his head. He kicked off his shoes, then dropped his pants and boxer briefs.

Larkin pulled in a shaky breath. He was magnificent. Tanned skin stretched tight over mounds of muscle lightly sprinkled with black hair. His torso narrowed slightly to his thick abs and his thighs flared back out in a way that made her want to sink her teeth into them. She stared, mute. There were no words to describe his erection, but there was every bit of evidence he felt the same desire for her.

"If you keep looking at me like that, this is going to be over way too soon." He inched closer to her, cupping her breasts in his hands. Lowering his head, he flicked his tongue over one tight nipple, sending a wash of awareness through her body in one swift kick.

"God." She let her head drop back.

"This is the closest I've ever been." He sucked a nipple into his mouth and the tight sensation shot to her center.

She gripped the back of his head, fisting his hair and pressing him tighter to her. His hands dropped to the top of her panties and slid beneath the band. He pushed them over her thighs, following the path with soft presses of his lips to her flushed skin.

A low groan reached her ears as she stepped from her flip flops and panties. The cool, velvety moss beneath her feet felt more luxurious than the finest silk sheets as she wiggled her toes deeper.

His hands glided up the back of her thighs, encouraging her to widen her stance. Then he dipped his head, placing a wet kiss along the inside of her knee. "Ryker?"

He slid his tongue along the sensitive skin of her inner thigh and she grabbed on to his shoulders to keep standing.

With a light nip at the juncture of her thigh and torso, he ground out, "Please don't tell me to stop."

She'd have grinned if she wasn't concentrating so hard on staying upright. "Don't stop." She massaged his shoulders, wanting to feel more of him but not wanting to distract him from what she hoped was his goal.

His hot tongue rubbed against her center and her knees buckled.

He tightened his grip on her ass as he continued to lick and suck. Every nerve ending in her body was primed and firing at will. She tilted her pelvis, encouraging him to continue, wanting more, *needing* more.

A tight ball of energy formed low in her stomach making her legs tremble. "I don't know if I—

"Stay with me, cupcake," he demanded as he continued tasting her.

She blinked, trying to clear her vision but everything around them glowed like stars in the night sky. Her body sang with each stroke of his tongue, and gruff demands or not, there was no way she'd be able to hang on much longer.

"Ryker." This time she wasn't asking, and he slid up her body, lifting her with him as he went. Before she caught up with the motion, he had her legs wrapped around his waist and stroked her sensitive folds with his hot, hard length.

She circled her arms about his neck, using his shoulders to leverage her body to move with him. Taking his mouth, she slid her tongue along his, reveling in every streak of pleasure that ran through her.

He supported her weight with one arm then slid his other hand between their bodies, gently circling her most sensitive place with his thumb.

"Now. I need to feel you now." She bit into the side of his neck, loving his taste, then soothing the area with her lips.

"You are so goddamn beautiful." He kissed her ravenously as he moved the large head of his shaft to her center, then slowly pushed in, inch by inch. His breath hissed out between his gritted teeth.

"Yes," she whimpered against his mouth as he filled her. Waves of pleasure pulsed as he buried himself to the hilt, and again as she rocked for him to slide out. They set up a rhythm, one perfectly matched with their tongues. Tasting his dark flavor, feeling him thrusting wide and deep inside her, enveloped by his scent, all of it threw her over the edge without warning. She bit into his shoulder as her release crashed over her in hard, hot, throbbing waves.

Gasping in pleasure, she slammed down again and again, her fingers gripping his relentless muscles. Her legs trembled and her body bowed back, straining against the sensation.

Ryker dropped his head to her breast, taking a nipple into his mouth as he too rode over the edge with a long, low groan.

His arms banded around her so effortlessly that she felt as though she were flying. The thought of crashing flitted about the ragged edges of reality, but she ignored the warning and focused on feeling alive—more than ever before.

As they fought to catch their breath, he kissed her mouth with slow, languorous strokes. "That was more than I—"

"I've never..." She didn't know how to finish the sentence as the reality of their situation slowly crept back in, destroying the lovely haze of paradise they'd created for themselves.

She'd never experienced something so intense, so wholly encompassing. And by the achingly tender look in his eyes, she'd have sworn that he felt it, too.

"Larkin, I think I'm fall—"

A sharp sting lit up one cheek of her ass. *Slap!*

"Shit." Larkin dropped her feet to the ground, then slapped at her arm this time. "Mosquitos. Ouch!" Another stung her arm.

At the same time, Ryker began to dance about as well. "What the hell? They came out of nowhere."

Grabbing her clothes and slipping her feet into her flip-flops, she swore. "Ohmygod! They're everywhere."

Ryker tucked his things under one arm and took her by the hand. "I have a bad feeling they were here all along." Pulling her behind him, they picked their way back through the woods, then broke out onto the lawn. The moon was high in the sky, making the lighter skin of his ass glow as they ran.

Larkin laughed.

Hard.

With humor lighting his eyes, he gazed back at her as they made their way up the front stairs of the house. "This is ridiculous."

She grinned. "We should have known better." Racing through the front door, they dropped their clothes on the tile then slammed the door behind them.

Seeing Ryker gloriously naked in the brighter light of the front hall sobered her. He was so much more than just a man trying to heal. He was larger than life, full of humor and passion, and had goals that were much different than her own. Despite the latter, he was the man she was losing her heart to.

And even Mother Nature was telling her it was a bad idea.

CHAPTER 13

*R*yker's chest burned with his effort to stop laughing, but it was more than the attack of the mosquitos, it was how effortlessly Larkin fit him. How perfectly her body had curved into his, how easily she took the abrupt end to their little excursion, even running naked with him across the grounds. "You are something."

Which was why he had to distance himself. This was what it was and nothing more. A means to blow off some steam, to ease the stress of both their situations. He'd simply needed a reminder.

And now he just needed to believe it.

She cleared her throat then looked down at herself. "I should probably put some clothes on." Scratching her arm, she picked up her dress.

"Now that would be a huge shame." He scratched at his thigh. Damn sons-o'-bitches got them good.

She rubbed at her cheek. "Ohmygod, they're all over." Turning toward the mirror, she groaned. "I have three bites on my face alone." As she looked over her arms and legs, she counted.

He slapped at his hip where a particularly large bite flared up. "Come on. Maxine has a trick that always helped me as a kid."

Leading the way up the stairs, his dick was well aware that she was still naked behind him and they were getting closer to his room. Apparently, not all of him cared about the damn mosquito bites. He flicked on the light of the master bathroom then sorted through the medicine cabinet. Grabbing a bottle and cotton swabs, he directed her to the sink.

"Sit up here."

She cleared her throat, gaining his attention. A deep red flush slowly made its way up her chest and neck. He followed the direction of her gaze to his now insistent hard-on.

On a bark of laughter, he pointed to the sink again. "Sit. I just had the best sex of my life, and the woman responsible is in my bathroom naked. Give me a break." He wiggled his brows. "Or another ten minutes."

She scooted her sweet ass onto the counter and he stepped between her thighs, unable to resist taking one more kiss, leaning into her just to see if she returned the favor.

She did.

His heart squeezed. Fuck.

The past few weeks had been changing her in a way he couldn't begin to understand, but he could see it. Her color was richer, her eyes not so hollow.

It was the Cape.

As much as he wished it were him.

"Quit distracting me," he commanded as he stepped back to assess the damage. Extending one of her legs out for his inspection, then the other, he lost count after fifty. "You're a tasty morsel." He threw her a leer before saturating the swab with tea tree oil.

She laughed, lightly nudging him on the shoulder. "Whoa...that's strong." She sniffed.

"You'll smell like this all night but the itching will subside. I promise." He dabbed one bite at a time, scouring every inch of her legs, torso, and arms. Her breasts were his favorite. Just large enough to fit snuggly in his palm, he was happy to report the mosquitoes had only gotten her twice on the one side.

A softness lit her eyes as she watched him, making him want to squirm.

"Thank you," she said.

He dipped his chin and cleared his throat.

"My turn." He handed her a newly saturated swab, and as she hopped from the sink, he slapped her ass.

"Hey!" She spun around. "That isn't necessarily the best decision considering you are now in my hands. Maybe I'll leave all the bites right in the center of your back untreated so they itch all night." She smirked at him with her hands on her hips.

And his heart gave a thump. This playful side of hers was going to be a problem.

"You wouldn't dare. Isn't it bad enough you're already trying to take the Cape?" He meant it as a joke but the light in her eyes immediately dimmed.

Not meeting his eyes, she told him to turn around.

He reached out for her hand. "Larkin. I was kidding."

She backed away, gesturing for him to turn. She dabbed at his back. "You're right. And we have to remember that."

Her gaze stayed downcast in the mirror but her hands were steady as she applied the oil to his bites. Once she finished, she tossed the swab in the trash. Slipping the dress over her head, she asked, "Did you grandfather set up multiple bees on the Cape on purpose?"

Ryker blinked at the change in conversation. His grandfather always had a reason for everything he did. He was a thinking man, a courteous one. A man Ryker aspired to be but always fell short. "He did. There are so many different flowers and plants--he wanted the same variety with the bees. He and Grandmother used to provide most of the honey sold around town."

"They don't now?"

He frowned. "When Grandfather died, Grandmother couldn't quite find the will to carry on some of the things they used to do, as if the memories were too much. It's a relief to see her spunk up these days, even if it is because of Judge Carter." He tried to hide his scowl.

"From what I hear, good ol' Teddy is quite the bear in—

He lunged, covering her mouth with his hand, and her eyes flew wide with mirth.

"Don't you dare finish that sentence." The idea of his grandmother in that way made his stomach sour. She made him cookies, for God's sake. And moonshine. There was that. "Promise me," he insisted.

She nodded and he slowly lowered his hand, but as she opened her mouth, he dove in to shut her up in a manner that promised the most effect.

Pulling her up tight against his naked chest, he slid his tongue along hers. He stroked his fingers through her hair and absorbed her sweet sigh that fell against his lips.

There was an indescribable relief, holding her in his arms.

Relief? That couldn't be right. But it was. He felt at ease with her close compared to the cold coil in his gut when he was on the Cape alone. He pressed a kiss to her forehead, skimmed his fingers down her neck before tucking his hands behind his back. "Did you leave the honey bars on my porch the other day?"

She nodded. "I thought you might like them."

"Why didn't you knock? I'd have shared."

"Oh?" She raised a brow, eyeing him up and down as he slid his legs into his jeans. "Like you were so gracious with the cupcakes?"

"I gave you one of each." He yanked on his shirt.

"You growled."

"I didn't."

She snorted at him then moved quickly through his room without looking at the bed.

Smart girl. If she knew what he was thinking, she'd be running.

He followed her, closing his hands to keep from reaching for her. But then gave in to the need screaming inside of him and grabbed for her hand. "Wait."

She reached up on tiptoe and pressed her mouth to his. He counted each second the kiss lasted.

"Stay. I make a mean waffle for breakfast." He hated the hope in his voice. He cleared his throat.

"I love waffles."

They slipped between the sheets of his bed. "I just want to hold you a little bit longer." Sliding his hand into the hair at the back of her head, he gripped it firmly and brought her mouth to his one more time. He kissed her, memorizing her taste, her texture. "I know this is complicated, but it isn't over."

She turned toward him in silent confirmation.

And he let himself take full pleasure in just holding her until her breaths eased into the easy rhythm of sleep.

. . .

*R*yker pressed both hands over his mouth to keep from screaming, to keep his ragged breathing from reaching his father's ears. This wasn't the first time his lungs burned with both the strain of running away and the cold, dark fear of pain. But in all his beatings, he'd never seen the look in his father's eyes be quite so bright with the thrill of the hunt.

The damp, pungent earth of the hollowed-out log filled his nose as he retreated into his hiding place as far as he could.

"Ryker! Come on out, boy!"

His father stomped about the woods just feet away, stopping every few minutes to listen for the slightest sound and watch for the slightest movement.

"It's gonna be worse for you the longer you hide. But I will find you!"

And his father wasn't lying. His last rant had sent both Ryker and his mother to the emergency room with the story that she had been carrying him down a flight of stairs and had fallen.

Trembling from the ice-cold fear trickling down his spine, Ryker shifted against the soft bark and an unmistakable *crack* destroyed the silence.

Suddenly his father's dark eyes, glinting from the light of the moon, peered menacingly at him from the opening of the log. "You shouldn't've hid, boy." His huge, work-worn hand grabbed the front of Ryker's shirt, tearing him from his shelter.

"No!" He shot up from the bed. Disoriented in the dark, he blindly swung away to stay out of reach of the fist flying toward his face.

"Ryker. It's okay. It's me." Larkin's sweet voice caressed his ears and he blinked, trying to make sense of what was happening.

"You were dreaming. It's not real." She stepped in front of him. "Look at me," she demanded as she lightly placed her hand against his chest. "I'm here."

His lungs burned. His heart slammed in his chest. Fear danced about his spine, but instead of hatred shining from his father's eyes, it was concern staring back at him from Larkin's.

He'd been dreaming. Fuck.

Running a hand through his hair, he dropped to the edge of the bed, willing his breath to ease. "I'm sorry."

She lowered carefully next to him. "You yelled. Like nothing I've ever heard before."

Shaking his head, he laid his hand on her thigh, the heat of her burning through the thin fabric of her dress. He traced the edge of her profile in the dark. The slope of her nose, the curve of her neck.

"A dream. My dad." He pulled in a steadying breath. "I used to have them all the time, but it's been awhile. I'm sorry for scaring you."

She scooted back to the pillows, patting the space next to her. "It's alright. I can't imagine how scared you must have been as a child."

As a child. As a man. When he dreamed, there was no difference. The fear was the same and very, very real.

And every inch of the Cape reminded him of how it had felt.

Joining her against the pillows, he pulled her into his embrace, and she laid her head against his chest.

"Your heart is beating so fast." She squeezed him.

"I'm fine." Of all the goddamn nights, he had to have the dream with her there to witness it.

Smooth.

"Do you want to talk about it?" She placed kisses against his neck.

"I think all of our talking is what probably triggered it in the first place."

She stiffened next to him, remaining silent for a moment. "I'm sorry."

"I'm not," he whispered, pushing her back and settling between her legs. "You're here."

He pressed into her and she sucked in a shaky breath, pulling him closer. "I'm here."

Blocking out the anger in his father's eyes and the sorrow in Larkin's, he took her mouth and sunk into the mind-altering effects of her taste.

He wanted to feel, to forget, to get lost in the pleasure they found in one another's arms.

So much for keeping his distance.

❧

"Thanks for coming in on a Saturday, gentlemen." Ryker stood at the head of the conference table in one of the meeting rooms on the top floor of the Cape Van Buren Library.

"I'll work on my wife's birthday as long as you're making me money," the first investor stated, then drew his brows together. "Which remains our concern, Van Buren."

Mitch handed out a one-page timeline report. "Gentlemen, this should ease any concerns you may have. We have acquired all the permits, the plans have been submitted to the city, and the contractors vetted. The only thing we're waiting on is the stay on the property to be lifted."

The second investor gave a cursory glance at the paper. His expression did not bode well for the meeting, nor did the tone of any of the men at the table.

The muscles at the back of Ryker's neck tightened painfully. He could not afford to have these investors drop out, nor did he have the time to find new ones. His leave from his job and life in New York was not indefinite. Not if he wanted to stay relevant anyway.

"Who is this Ms. Sinclair that initiated the stay in the first place?" The first investor tapped a finger on her name at the bottom of the page.

"She's a local conservationist who's very familiar with the property."

"A conservationist?" The second investor sounded disgusted. "Just what we need, another goddamn tree-hugger getting in the way. I bet she gets her panties in a bind every time one of those pathetic animal commercials comes on. An ignorant hindrance of progress if you ask me."

Ryker stepped forward, his fingers curled into fists at his sides, but Mitch placed a grounding hand on his shoulder.

The asshole investor had no idea how close he'd just come to choking on his tongue.

"Ms. Sinclair is doing her job. And I'll do mine. You have nothing to worry about."

The first investor laughed. "If we had nothing to worry about, we wouldn't be here, now would we?" He shifted in his chair, bouncing his gut off the table. "Van Buren, let me say this as simply as possible. Get the stay removed. If you can't handle some twit conservationist, how the hell do you expect us to trust you handling our money?"

Goddamn, self-important, chauvinistic fuckheads. No one in New York would ever talk to him in that tone. As a matter of fact, the investors who knew him clamored to work with him. The only reason he even had Mitch approach these asses was to stay local. Local investors meant local profit and economy, which would go a long way with the board. But these bastards were making it damn hard.

"My work speaks for itself. You have the timeline, gentlemen. If you have any other questions, call Mitch." He dismissed them and moved toward the back of the room before he lost his shit and told them where to stick their wads of green.

He'd make sure it was so far up their asses they tasted it.

Mitch quickly stepped in, assuring the men they'd hear from them the next week, all the while making apologies for Ryker.

As soon as the door closed, he spun around. "Don't ever apologize for me."

Mitch eyed him with a disgusted look of his own. "Step off your over-entitled pedestal, you prick. You're counting on those men to stay in the game. You don't do that by dismissing them like schoolchildren."

"They're assholes."

"Yes, they are, but they're the assholes who are going to make it possible for you to finally free yourself of the Cape." Mitch slammed his hand on the table. "What the hell is your problem?"

Larkin's green eyes flashed in his head. He didn't like the way they talked about her at all, but he wasn't about to tell his buddy that. He'd never hear the end of it and Mitch would go running to Maxine before he even finished the sentence. How the hell did putting his past to rest become so complicated?

"Don't tell me you're pissed over what they said about Larkin?"

Ryker gave him a hard stare.

"Dude. They're prehistoric cavemen with pockets of money. They don't know anything more about Larkin than the fact she's a woman and in their way. But what the fuck? Since when do you let shit like that affect your business sense?" Mitch gathered his notes then shoved them in his bag.

"Look." He shoved in the chairs around the tables. "We have to get that stay lifted. Have you thought of anything we can use to win our case?"

The honey bees and Larkin's assertion that there were so many varieties on the Cape came to mind. Destroying them would destroy him, not to mention his chances of keeping the Cape. But she didn't know that. She assumed they'd all go, which explained why she'd been studying them yesterday. He'd gone out to clear some honey but had found her standing there, unreal in the soft light of the forest, his bees humming in the background.

And all he could think was that he needed to touch her.

Now that he had, he saw it as the mistake it was, but damn if he wouldn't do it again. The biggest problem was that she deserved more than a jackass of a man loaded down with baggage, too broken to love and too determined to get out of town.

"I do have some ideas but let me figure a few things out first. I'll fill you in and see what your take is on Monday."

Mitch's shoulders eased. "Good. Good." He moved to the door. "Are you stopping at the festival? Let me rephrase that…when you stop at the festival, so my mother and your grandmother don't make me hunt you down, make sure to watch out for the triplets."

A streak of fear sliced down Ryker's back at the mention of the three twenty-something sisters from the North Cove. Their dad was the high school football coach and if he ever caught anyone even thinking about his daughters he'd as soon cut their balls off as shake their hand.

Mitch slapped a hand to his chest. "They are gorgeous, legal, and all three smart as shit, but even I cross the road to pass them on the street. Coach Dawson scares the hell out of me. But Candy said they heard you were in town and are hoping to 'catch up.'" He made air quotes with his fingers.

Ryker furrowed his brow. "Catch up how? They don't know me at all. I was a senior when they were in eighth grade." He shuddered.

Mitch saluted then took off through the door.

"Wait, who's Candy? And what the hell happened to Cindy?" He scrubbed his hand over his face. Fuck. Why in the hell did he care? Mitch went through women like water through a colander.

Left in the silence of the conference room, he glanced out the large, arched windows that faced Garden Parkway NW. He could see the crowds gathering through the brick walkways that ran between the shops across the street. The North Garden was just on the other side. Which meant Larkin was less than a block away. He had to make an appearance and get the hell out before the woman's nearness did him in. She already saw too much as it was. He was no less than mortified that she'd witnessed one of his damn nightmares. Then the way she comforted him…

Larkin.

He couldn't get the image of her, the feel of her in his arms, out of his head.

127

Her silky skin made promises with every inch he explored. The way her breath caught when he kissed her always sent him over the edge, and his dick grew hard just to prove a point.

He yanked on his tie and forced himself to focus on the matter at hand.

The Cape.

Those damn old fucks had no idea what they were talking about. There was nothing to handle when it came to the Cape. The property was his and would stay that way.

Larkin may have conservation on her side, but Ryker had ownership and cold hard business savvy on his.

He cracked his neck against the mounting pressure.

He was more than capable of handling his business—the idea that they questioned him burned his ass. It was enough to have his grandmother disappointed and his father laughing. Their questions were almost enough to push him over the edge and demand they get the hell out.

And he would have if he didn't think they'd help his case. In the end, he needed them to move forward.

Past the Cape.

And in the end, past Larkin.

He was never meant to stay in town, or with her. So why the hell did the thought leave his gut churning with loss and regret?

CHAPTER 14

$\mathcal{C}$ape Van Buren was at its best during the Garden Festival. All sides of the town were in full bloom, not just the flowers but the people, too. It was as if the citizens themselves were in competition with the potted planters hanging from windows up and down the historic brick buildings of Van Buren Boulevard.

Larkin walked the stone sidewalks along the perimeter of the North Gardens and admired the Mavens' handiwork. The garden looked as though a flock of jeweled peacocks had settled home for the rest of the summer. Bright turquoise, glistening emerald, and radiant ruby burst in a spray of flowered feathers from each bush.

"This looks spectacular, Maxine." Slipping her arm around her sassy friend, she gave the older woman a squeeze. "I think we've outdone ourselves."

Maxine nodded, her silver strands settling effortlessly back in perfect order. "Of course it is. The Mavens are a special lot, not to mention Claire turned out to be a godsend."

A small band tightened around Larkin's chest, but she appreciated the fact it had been less than two weeks since her overture to Claire. She was making progress. "Who knew she was so creative? The interactive stations she created for the kids are amazing. And the little pinwheels they get to collect at each stop are already a huge hit," she said, waving her hand at a group of elementary students running through the grounds and spinning their prizes, their laughter floating just above the general hum of conversation.

Maxine looked her over. "You look different. Better. Brighter."

Larkin knew a flush raced up her neck.

So did her friend and her eyes lit with interest. "A lot brighter." She wiggled her brows.

Larkin threw out her hands. "No, no. I've just...it's felt really good to work toward something worthy, something for Archer. The special plants and animals on the cape are a gift."

"Uh huh..." Maxine winked. "Does this something worthy happen to be about six-foot-four with a dark scowl and a heart of gold?"

Larkin laughed. "Only you'd describe Ryker like that." Actually, it was a perfect description. He did have a heart of gold when it came to his grand-mother, to others' emotions, just not the Cape. Which was why he so often did have a scowl. One she wanted to kiss right off his face.

Maxine clucked. "Something on your mind?"

Clearing her throat, she slid her arm through Maxine's as they walked. "Listen, when I get the Cape declared for conservation, I want to open a community outreach that provides all sorts of resources for the town. Everything from arts to environ-ment to health and wellness..." She trailed off as her heart picked up its beat. It would change Van Buren in ways she could only imagine until she made it happen. That's what this new opportunity had taught her. It was time for her to make her life happen, not merely exist within its confines of loneliness and heartache.

She stopped and faced her friend. "I want Claire to help me with the art component. She has a real talent that I'm not sure she even recognizes. I think it could help her heal." The young woman needed a way to find a life herself. She hadn't opened up to Larkin yet, but it was clear that she hadn't moved on from her loss either. It was time they both did.

Smooth fingers settled on her arm and Larkin looked into Maxine's troubled face.

With a small tap that set her antique bracelets tinkling, she tilted her head. "You know you aren't responsible. And it wasn't only John's fault either. Both men made decisions that day that took everything from you and Claire."

Larkin looked around the gardens, the families laughing, mothers smiling down into the shining eyes of their children. John's face popped into her mind and instead of numbness, a fist of rage grew in her stomach.

"I think I might hate him," she whispered.

Maxine squeezed her hand. "It's about time, my dear."

Larkin stopped breathing and shock lit through her chest. "I doubt it's a good thing. I mean, I can't hate Archer's father. It's not right." Knowing it didn't mean she wasn't feeling it.

"It's better than the nothing you've been feeling. It's real. And I'd hate the man who was responsible for my son's death, too, until I found a way to work through that into some sort of forgiveness, or at least acknowledgment."

Holding Maxine's gaze, she struggled to find the right words. Surely, she shouldn't focus on hating him but at that moment, if she were honest, that was exactly what she felt.

"There you are!"

Maxine and Larkin turned to find Shelly Anne walking toward them with two cups from the Flat Iron Coffeehouse in her hands. She glanced at her concession stand, set up at the end of a row, with a small wrinkle in her nose. "My high school students need to liven up over there. It's like a morgue. Who wants coffee from a place full of dead people?"

"Shelly Anne, it's a coffee stand, not a disco," Maxine chided with a shake of her head.

Shelly Anne scoffed. "Shows what you know."

Maxine looked their new arrival up and down, then eyed her with suspicion but sniffed at the air all the same.

The freshly brewed aroma drifted on the breeze and gently wafted to their noses as though heaven sent. Larkin couldn't resist the pull herself.

"What are you doing over here? This is nothing but a sorry attempt at gaining some intel, Shelly Anne."

The two women stood nose to nose in silence. Maxine, in her nautical striped shirt and walking shorts topped off with deck shoes and gold jewelry, looked like she'd stepped right off the boat Ryker had been working on the other day. Shelly Anne looked positively earthy in her usual bohemian-style dress and waist-length hair pulled back into a long, silver-streaked braid. No one would ever guess she'd been a Studio 54 dancer back in her day.

Suddenly both women burst out laughing and Shelly Anne handed over the coffees.

Maxine took an appreciative sip. "Oh, God. Your coffee is divine." She narrowed her gaze. "But if you ever tell Evette, I'll call you a liar and still come into the cafe the next day."

Shelly Anne wrinkled her nose. "Please. Even Evette knows my coffee is the best in town. I know every delivery we make. She's one of my best customers. It's hard to hide anything in Cape Van Buren."

The woman tossed her long braid back over her shoulder and pinned her gaze on Larkin. "Speaking of hiding things, what's this I hear you've been spending time out on the Cape?"

Janice joined them with a harried look on her face, her red curls bouncing. "I think those kids might be the death of me yet."

Larkin took the interruption as divine intervention and waved off. "I need to go find Claire real quick. Thanks for the coffee, Shelly Anne." She lifted her cup and slipped away before she had to answer any more questions. Usually walking away from the group like that would guarantee she'd be the topic of discussion. But Shelly Anne and Janice would have to do the usual North versus South challenge dance before they got back to talking.

Fingers crossed that by then they'd move on to less volatile topics. Just thinking about Ryker made her heart pound in an all too delicious way. She gave her visible mosquito bites a cursory glance—the tea tree oil took away the itching and the swelling, so at least now her late-night, best-sex-she'd-ever-imagined adventure was simply dotted across her body in tiny pinpoints instead of swollen red welts.

Talk about volatile. She'd never forget the panic and fear on his face after his nightmare. She couldn't imagine her own son ever experiencing the horror Ryker had. Really seeing the effects of what he'd gone through made what she had to do so much harder.

She was falling for a man that she could never have.

When he'd asked her to stay, she couldn't say no. But she'd left before he woke. A hint of self-preservation still remained.

Once she'd escaped outside, she'd turned back twice, then swore at herself all the way home for being an idiot.

The more time she spent with Ryker, the worse it would feel to lose him in the end. She scoffed. How could she lose something she'd never had?

But apparently she could fall in love with him...despite her best efforts to keep him at arm's length.

Spotting Claire on the opposite side of the peacock garden, she waved her down.

Claire joined her willingly, if a tad warily. But it was progress.

Larkin pulled in a deep breath as she approached. Claire stiffened but fell into step.

"What do you want?" She sounded tired.

Larkin smiled. "I want a chance to talk, but I also want to see what we're up against this year. Let's go check out the South Garden."

"Oh, no, you don't!" Evette waved them down. "You two aren't going anywhere. We're about to begin the Posey Planting Pair-Up, and we need a few more contestants."

Larkin threw up her hands. "No way. Not interested."

"Like that matters. Here..." Maxine handed her a piece of rope, and Larkin eyed it with unease. How appropriate since there was no getting out of this. She was right and tight tied up.

The emcee, none other than Judge Carter himself, told everyone to find their partners.

Kids and adults quickly claimed their mates then headed to the starting line.

A broad-shouldered man in an opened shirt and the jacketless remains of a suit strode toward the garden with his dark eyes fixed to the ground.

"Ryker." The breathless tone of Larkin's voice sounded ridiculous to her ears. The man's mouth had been places she could barely think about without her knees buckling, and now she sounded like a schoolgirl with her first crush. Good God.

His head snapped up and his eyes focused on her with that intense look he always had, as if trying to figure out a difficult puzzle.

"Larkin." His gaze darted to Claire and Maxine, and he nodded, but he kept walking.

The brush off tightened her throat and she swallowed hard past it.

"Get back here, boy, and where's Mitch? His mother's looking for him." Maxine demanded.

Ryker glanced at the sky then back to his grandmother. "I'll warn him."

She glared.

"I'll tell him. I was just stopping by to say good luck but I have to get home."

Judge Carter joined them. "Here you go, Van Buren." He shoved a rope in Ryker's hand. "Let's see how you and Ms. Sinclair do when you're on the same team."

"What? No. I'm just leaving, Judge." Ryker's eyes held a bit of a wild look. Like when a cornered animal feared the predator.

Larkin would have laughed except she was pretty sure she was the predator to him. "I don't have time either. Claire and I were just headed over to check out the competition."

Claire laughed. "No way. I'm not missing this."

So much for any hope of camaraderie.

Janice walked up with Mitch in tow. "Look who I found trying to skate past the concession stands." She shoved her son toward Claire. "We've got the last match, Judge."

Mitch's face blanched white as he looked from Claire to the rope his mother was handing him, his blue eyes wide and begging her to stop. "Oh, hell no."

"Watch your mouth, young man." Maxine reprimanded.

He swung toward her. "What? At the Cape you said—

Ryker slapped his buddy on the back. "If I have to, you have to, *sucker*." Revenge replaced his earlier fear, though Larkin didn't quite understand the aggressive competition between men.

Mitch took the challenge, throwing his arm over a surprised Claire's shoulders. She stood frozen, as if maybe no one would notice her if she just didn't move.

Ryker turned his attention back to Larkin but instead of the playful mood she was hoping for, he was serious. "Here." He motioned for her to place her leg next to his, then he tied them together.

All the contestants had their hands bound behind their backs. The object of the game was to use a small beach bucket, shovel, and their teeth to carry soil from a bin to a table twenty feet away. At the table, they had to fill a pot and plant a posey so it stood upright. Whoever finished first won.

Ryker and Larkin were up against Mitch and Claire, as well as a few teen/parent match-ups, and one of the triplets with Dr. Stanton's son, Max.

Mitch nudged Ryker. "Told you they were here."

Ryker glanced at the tall, blonde sister then scowled at his buddy.

Larkin had no idea what that could be about, and she had no idea which sibling the beautiful young woman happened to be.

"What's he talking about?"

"Nothing. Just trying to get under my skin. Apparently, Coach Dawson's daughters are on the market."

"And they're interested in you?" She said, not meaning for her tone to come across so surprised.

"What's that supposed to mean?" He glowered at her as they hobbled to the starting line.

"Nothing, they're just pretty young is all. And you're a bit—

"What?" His question cut through the air just as Judge Carter waved the North Cove Maven's flag, starting the race.

Together, they bent forward to grab the handle of the bucket with their teeth.

"A bit grouchy," she finished, then clamped onto her side of the handle. The heat of his big, hard body enveloped her, making the comfortable, seventy-degree day feel sweltering.

With his brow furrowed, he glared at her but couldn't say anything. It was kind of perfect, and everything Larkin could do not to laugh outright. They lined up on either side of the potting soil table then, working side by side, dragged their bucket through the dirt until it was full. Carefully, they hobbled toward their potting table, finding an easy rhythm that they naturally fell into.

The crowds cheered and clapped, calling out encouragement to their favored contestants, but Larkin was more aware of the strained sound of Ryker's breathing and grunts of effort. Her toes curled as images of his other very well-performed efforts came to mind.

Dumping the soil into the planter was a bit more challenging. She continued to hold the handle of the bucket while he released it and used his nose to lift the bottom until the dirt emptied into the planter.

"I'm not grouchy."

She raised a brow in disbelief.

"Yeah, well, someone is trying to take my home from me."

When they got back to the potting table, she dropped the bucket. "You don't look at it as home…you look at it as a profit. There's a big difference. And why are you being such an ass? Last night you were offering me waffles, today it's nothing but attitude."

They retrieved the bucket and repeated the same process two more times.

Finally, back at the potting table, they faced a row of tulips with intact bulbs.

She carefully lifted the stem with her teeth then bent her head sideways until she was able to slide the bulb through the loose soil. Ryker held a small plastic shovel between his teeth and packed the soil tight. As she carefully released the tulip, she held her breath. It leaned, but only a bit.

"We have a winner!" Judge Carter's announcement pealed through the speakers.

The unexpected win lit Ryker's eyes in a way she'd never seen before. He let out a victory cry then took her mouth with his.

The world stopped.

His heat enveloped her, the smooth glide of his lips branded her, and his taste left her dizzy and drunk. Their arms were still tied behind their backs so she pressed in closer.

Reality trickled in with the sudden silence around them.

"Shit." He sucked in a breath and tried to back away but their legs were still tethered. The sudden tug had her rearing back, then overcorrecting forward, falling against his chest once again.

"We need to quit meeting like this, cupcake," he whispered.

She closed her eyes against her rising panic. "This is not good."

They'd kissed in front of the whole town.

"We have a complicated situation," he said in a softer tone, but a split second later his gaze shuttered.

She lifted her chin, resisting the guilt weighing heavy on her shoulders.

Maxine cleared her throat and removed the rope from Ryker's hands then moved over to Larkin, her eyes shining brighter than ever before.

"Grandmother, don't say a word," he growled.

"I don't have to." She all but preened as she assisted them.

He rubbed his wrist, holding Larkin's gaze. "And it's not getting any better." Without another word, he left the playing field in the direction of the square.

The rope dropped from Larkin's wrists and she stared after him.

Maxine stepped up beside her with both pieces of rope in her hands. "What was that all about?"

She shook her head, ignoring the real question. "What do you think?" She crossed her arms over her chest as she watched his large figure disappear between the buildings.

"The Cape." Maxine handed her the rope. "Judge wasn't wrong you know." The smile on her face full of satisfaction.

"What's that?"

"You two do make a very good team."

In another time, another life, the statement would have warmed her heart and sent it skipping with possibility, but now it left her unbearably sad.

Maxine caught sight of something over Larkin's shoulder and smiled. Spinning her gold bands on her fingers, she said, "I need to grab Teddy and walk him past the Garden Festival judging table."

"You don't think that's going to help, do you? Besides, you want to win because you deserve it."

Maxine snapped. "Damn right I do—on both accounts."

"You're really enjoying living across from the square. There's so much color in your face, almost a glint in your eye I don't think I noticed before."

Her friend grabbed her hand. "Honey, until recently, you weren't noticing much. But yes, I do love living in the city."

The city. Cape Van Buren wasn't a small town but it certainly wasn't the size of a city. At least not the size of the one Ryker came from—the one he'd go back to.

She shook the thought from her head and chuckled as Maxine claimed Teddy at the winner's circle. Mitch and Claire sported second place ribbons and the teen/parent combo happily claimed third. But it was the Dawson triplet who looked as though she'd won first place. She was wrapped around Max's arm like a blood pressure cuff.

And he didn't seem to mind one bit.

Claire joined her, showing off her ribbon. "I can't believe we came in second. I don't think I've ever won anything before." She raised her brows. "But more important, I can't believe Ryker kissed you in front of everyone." The look of shock and awe on the woman's face made Larkin want to disappear before anyone else said anything.

She could already feel the heat scorching her neck and cheeks.

"Well, if you ask me, Van Buren has the right of it. After that little show, I'd have cut and run myself." Claire laughed then sobered at Larkin's serious expression. "Not the friendliest guy I've ever met."

Shaking her head, Larkin peeked back over her shoulder. "Actually, he's growing on me. But something must have happened." He wasn't happy and the only thing that would make him that short toward her was something regarding the Cape. A small fissure of anticipation shot through her, followed by a swift clutch of guilt. If he'd found out information that made him upset, it might be really good for her.

"Whatever you say," Claire shrugged.

Janice, Evette, and Maxine were chatting and pointing their way with an urgency that scared Larkin more than bees.

"Shit." She grabbed Claire's hand, heading down the walk. "Keep your head down and don't stop no matter what you hear."

Claire pulled back on her hand but Larkin refused to let go.

They made their way across Garden Parkway NW to the square and then over Garden Parkway SE and passed the Flat Iron Coffeehouse. Ducking down one of the narrow alleyways, they walked toward the bright light at the end of the long, narrow buildings. Paved in brick and spotted with wrought iron gates and windows, the walkways looked like something out of an old coastal storybook. Larkin loved the potted plants that dotted the way, and now and then, the rows of brick opened for the hollow of a doorway. Finally, they stepped back out into the full sun of the South Gardens.

"Whoa." Claire stopped and scanned the scene. Just as many adults and children as in the North Gardens walked along the stone sidewalks and ran through the grasses. Concession stands lined the north perimeter, and a remote-controlled boat race was going on in the small pond on the south side. "They pulled off more than I thought possible."

Larkin smiled at the large lollipops and gumdrops. The South Cove Madams had turned their garden into a candy-land of sorts and, of course, there were plenty of sweets for the kiddos.

"I'm not surprised. As much as Maxine and the ladies like to cluck, the Madams are a talented bunch. And when push comes to shove, they get things done."

"I can't believe they keep a feud going that began so long ago. I bet they can't even remember what started it." Claire rolled her blue eyes.

"Speaking of feuds." Larkin trailed her fingers along a canary yellow lollipop made of dahlias. "I have a proposition for you." She turned and put her finger up to keep the stubborn woman quiet.

Claire snapped her mouth closed but narrowed her eyes.

"I'm working to have the Cape conserved. It was my little boy's favorite place in the world." Despite the pang of longing in her heart, she couldn't help the smile that spread her lips wide. The vision of Archer running to the well on their Wednesday trips always warmed her from the inside out.

Claire's eyes wavered.

They picked their way through the garden, passing Jolly Ranchers made of roses and gummy bears of purple asters. "I plan on opening a community outreach of sorts on the Cape."

Claire shook her head. "How are you so sure you're going to win? Van Buren is the rightful owner."

A sick weight grew heavier in her stomach. "I know, but the Cape is a very special place with animals and plants that aren't found anywhere else in this area. If he develops it, they'll all be destroyed."

"Your memories will be destroyed."

Larkin blinked a few times. "Yes," she whispered.

"I don't have any to begin with."

Reaching out toward her, Larkin wanted to argue. But the truth was, she wouldn't give up her memories of Archer for anything, no matter how much pain came with them. They were everything to her now. And Claire's had been snatched from her before they even existed.

"I want you to help me make new memories, beautiful ones with more kids than we'd know what to do with."

Claire tucked her blond hair back behind her ears with an impatient jerk. "What are you talking about?"

Larkin plucked a lollipop from one of the bowls set up around the garden, then handed it to her new, tentative friend. "You and I can help each other heal by giving the kids in this town the Cape. Some place to go to learn how to draw, learn why lighthouses were made, or maybe all the things honey is good for."

Claire shook her head. "But why would you want me to help you?"

That was a good question. She had wanted to reach out since the fateful day of the accident but never knew how, and Claire hadn't wanted her to, that had been abundantly clear. They'd been an awful reminder to each other for so long but it was time to change that.

"Together, we can find a purpose in this town, make a new life that we aren't always hiding from."

Claire finally took the lollipop she'd offered. She turned the sucker slowly in her hand, eyeing it as it spun. "Where would we hold these…classes?"

"That's what I'm thinking. The house Maxine used to live in would make a perfect community center."

"You mean Ryker's home?"

Larkin lifted her chin. "Yes." Though her voice was low, her answer was firm.

Claire pulled in a shaky breath. "Then you better save the Cape."

CHAPTER 15

*R*yker breathed deeply, taking in the scent of damp earth and moss as he collected honey frames and replaced them with empty ones. The hives were thriving—all of them. Regardless of Larkin's fears and his grandmother's doubt. The hum around him was calm and low and soothed him in a way he hadn't experienced in a long time.

Not since working with his grandfather.

He paused, picturing Stuart in the very bee suit he was wearing. As a kid, he'd tried it on a time or two and it had been ten times too big, but now fit just right.

It had been a few days since he'd been a complete ass and then kissed Larkin in front of the whole town. But the meeting had gone about as badly as it could have, reinforcing his need to focus, and then he'd gotten distracted by the unexpected win. And once her lips responded under his, inciting him to deepen the kiss, he'd promptly forgotten they were in the middle of town. Fuck.

In the end, he'd do it again. If he wanted to kiss Larkin, goddamnit, he would.

He was tired of the judgments, of being second-guessed, by not only the people he worked with but his family and friends. They should know him better. They should trust him.

But the itch between his shoulder blades made it impossible for him to hide from the truth.

They didn't know him anymore. He hadn't let them.

As the tightness collected again at the back of his neck, he dropped his shoulders and closed his eyes. Inside the hood, with the bees flying about him, it was as if he were in a world all to himself. His muscles eased and his breathing came easy. It was a world he preferred over interfering friends with good intentions or entitled investors with more ignorance than sense.

Using his lifting tool, he pulled up another honey frame. The burr comb had built up a bit, and he scraped it from the edges.

He was an idiot. He might as well have kissed her on national television for the drama it stirred up. He was surprised he hadn't already seen the headline, CAPE VAN BUREN'S GRUMPIEST BACHELOR AND THE TREE-HUGGING WIDOW, splashed across *The Van Buren Tribune*.

His phone hadn't stopped ringing and both Mitch and Maxine had come pounding on his door.

Somehow, he'd managed to see no one for three days. He'd counted himself lucky.

And his bees were thriving. That was a miracle.

Regardless of what his father thought, his grandfather would be proud. And he let that fact ease the stress of the rest.

Larkin's observations on the different bee populations were spot on and surprising. She was a conservationist, sure, but she was scared shitless of the bees. Yet, she noticed. And she cared.

Regardless how he developed the land, he planned to protect the bees. He might be an ass but he was an intelligent one. And it might just be the angle that would win him his rightful place on the estate.

Replacing the lid on top of the super that held the Italian bees, he turned his attention to the gentler Carniolan hive. A flash of rich, honey-colored hair caught his eye, and he straightened. Larkin sat on the bench quietly watching him, settled in with her legs crossed at the ankles and leaning back as if she'd been there for a while. His body tightened in the now familiar sensual pull of wanting her. He wanted to hold her in his arms as much as his heart warned him to stay away.

"You're enjoying yourself." She looked pleased. The woman was an enigma.

"I am." And that said a lot for anything having to do with the Cape. "My grandfather taught me everything I know. The bees do as well. They're resourceful and tough, yet they make one of the sweetest foods on earth."

Grabbing his frames of honey, he walked toward her.

She stood from the bench with a bit of a crazed look as he approached. A look that made him want to shield her from all the bad in the world. Then her green eyes raked over him, and his body responded, but it was obvious her focus had more to do with watching out for any hitch-hiking bees than the way he filled out his suit. Fuck. He had to get a hold of himself.

He chuckled, low and raspy. "Relax, they'll all fly back to the hive."

She pulled in a breath as she nodded, drawing his gaze to the swell of her breasts peeking from the top of the deep V in her t-shirt. The cooler day had her curvy ass encased in a pair of dark washed jeans, and he thanked Mother Nature for being so accommodating. Then promised himself he'd get her off his property as quickly as possible no matter how much his hands wanted to mold to her backside.

He removed his hood, gingerly turning it to inspect for any of his winged friends.

"I just finished up along the north shoreline. I think I have everything I need."

He dipped his chin and brushed past her. "Great."

Breaking out of the woods and onto the lawn, he called over his shoulder. "Can you see yourself out?"

But she followed him to the house and into the back mudroom where his grandfather had the honey extractor set up. "Why are you so mad at me?"

He set the frames on the counter and plugged in the electric knife he'd use to remove the wax capping so the honey would flow once the frames were in the extractor.

He wanted to tell her about his meeting, about the jackass investors, and all his frustrations. But she couldn't be that person for him.

"Tell me about Archer."

She stiffened, her fingers flying to the locket resting over her heart. Staring at the floor, she pulled in a breath and sat at the small table next to the extractor. "He was my bright light. I don't understand what you want to know."

143

He lined up the knife along the short side of one frame then slowly slid it down the length, exposing the raw honey.

"What did he love about the Cape?"

She laughed quietly. It wasn't in humor, but the kind when something hits home bittersweet.

"He loved Maxine and the way she saw the world with such spunk. She made him laugh. We'd do picnics out on the lawn by the lighthouse and work on puzzles. His favorite was one of the lighthouse itself. Your grandmother had it made."

"She's thoughtful like that. Finding connections, knowing what's important to people."

Larkin nodded, staring off as if watching a moment unfold on a projection screen. "He made a wish at the well...every visit. It was always about me or Maxine, his daddy. That we'd be well and one day be as good at puzzles as he was." She chuckled softly.

"He had a rule, you know." Her eyes welled with unshed tears. She sniffed. "With every wish, the penny had to reach the bottom before it was spoken for it to come true."

An uncomfortable pressure settled on his chest. That must have been what she'd whispered about the day she'd offered to buy the property.

She swallowed hard on a trembling smile. "His dad came to pick him up and take him home the day of the car accident. So I could meet up with Blayne in town. I remember saying goodbye, the way his hair smelled sweet from his shampoo and felt warm from the sun. I can still feel him against my chest as he hugged me goodbye. The weight of him, the sound of his footsteps when he'd run down the hall in the mornings to crawl into bed with me and snuggle." A tear broke over her lower lashes and ran down her cheek.

He set the frame and knife aside then washed his hands, watching her intently as she continued to speak.

"His dad had a bad temper and always lost his cool on the road. I should never have—"

"He was his father. There's nothing you should or should not have done." He moved to stand in front of her. It was the very reason his grandmother's hands had been so tied when he'd been a child. He refused to admit the abuse was happening in order to protect his grandmother, so the authorities had nothing to go on but speculation.

Gripping her hands in his, he kissed her knuckles. "It wasn't your fault. Period."

She glanced at him, her lashes in a ray of wet spikes. "I should have protected him."

Which was why she felt the need to protect the Cape.

He got it.

But if she'd only trust him, believe in him, she'd see his plans wouldn't destroy it. He'd be giving families what she and Archer had with Maxine. A magical place to make memories.

There was no telling her that though. Part of dealing with loss was taking it step by step. Her mission was part love of the land, part love of Archer, and part a need of not being powerless. If she didn't try, she'd never get past it.

So he got it.

But he had to do the same for himself.

He cupped her face then ran a thumb under each eye, wiping away her tears. "Tell me a good memory."

She rewarded him with a watery smile. "Once, when Henry Stull, the old lighthouse keeper, was visiting as he always did after your grandfather passed, Archer challenged us to a puzzle-off. I think we'd attended one too many Project Community Unity events downtown."

Twisting her hands in her lap, she continued, "Whoever could finish their puzzle first got to pick the flavor of ice cream for after dinner." She shook her head. "Your grandmother is a great cook, by the way."

He nodded, remaining quiet.

She pulled in a breath. "We had no plans for ice cream but it was Archer's way to make sure we did. Needless to say, even with my sweet boy letting his older friends work together on a puzzle, he won. He'd thrown his hands so high in the air, you'd think he'd just won the Super Bowl."

She stood from the table, smoothing her t-shirt down the front. "He was always having little wins like that. Finding ways to get ice cream, rides on the four-wheeler, play time in the lighthouse. He knew how to work us with that smile and his innocence. We were helpless to resist."

He pulled her into his chest. She stiffened at first, then melted into him in such a way he never wanted to let her go. He was at ease with her in his arms. No tension in his shoulders, no pounding in his head. Just a calm peace in her presence, which made no sense when she was fighting him for his land. But there it was.

He loved her. God help him. He loved the one woman who could get in the way of him righting his past. And he could get in the way of righting her future. They were at a crossroads where no one would win. Not really.

And he wasn't good for her. He had so many demons that the devil himself was too scared to fuck with him. But more, he could never give her what she needed. He couldn't give her the Cape, or a family, or all of himself. He hadn't been whole since the first time he saw his dad punch his mother in the face, since the time that same fist smashed into his own.

Clearing his throat, he kissed the top of her head. "He sounds like a mini version of you, cupcake. He made people smile, made them want to make his dreams come true."

She tilted her face up. "No one wants to make my dreams come true," she whispered.

"I do." But wanting to and being able to were very different bed partners.

He brushed his lips over hers, once, twice. His body tightened at the caress of her mouth, but his heart cracked open wide. The fear of wanting her, of losing her, of never having her made his chest ache.

Sinking into the kiss, he memorized her taste in that moment. With the scent of honey heavy in the air, mixing with her own sweetness, there was nothing more he needed. He pulled back, kissed her nose, then her forehead.

"Come help me."

Her eyes widened. "With what?"

He led her out to the back porch where he'd set up borders to mimic slabs of river rock. "A few sections of the patio needed to be repaired. They're poured cement."

"But why are you fixing them if you're just going to tear the whole place down?"

He shook his head, part in exasperation, part in acceptance. "Who ever said I was tearing it down?"

"Well, you implied it."

"No, you inferred it."

She frowned but stepped to his side. They worked in silence, adding water to a bag of cement he'd poured into a wheelbarrow then, one by one, filling each bordered section and smoothing the top. There was no denying how smoothly they operated. He'd move one way, she'd complete the action in another. Their efforts were completely in sync.

Finally, when the last mock stone was poured, they studied their creations, kneeling side by side. "Here." He scooted over, indicating for her to come closer. He placed both of his hands on top of the last stone and pressed. Carefully peeling his hand back up, he grabbed hers.

"What are you doing?"

He sighed. "Just trust me, okay, cupcake?"

She raised a brow but nodded.

"Regardless of what happens, each of us will have left a mark." He encouraged her to spread her fingers as he had, then placed each of her hands inside the print of his own. His chest tightened at just how perfectly they fit in his.

He knelt behind her, his arms around her body, and as he lifted her hands from the cement, he slid his fingers back up the length of her arms.

"You're getting cement all over me." Her voice wavered, but she continued to stare at the handprints they'd made. The sound made him feel all kinds of complicated things, so he shoved any possibility from his head and let his body take over.

"Then let me wash it off." He answered gruffly. He rose, offering his hand. His relief was swift as she slid hers into it and allowed him to pull her to her feet.

They made their way through the house and to his bathroom in silence. She had a smudge of cement on her nose and a little on a few strands of hair that had escaped her ponytail to flutter about her face. She was so beautiful, delicate, with the strength of the iron used to set the foundations in the lighthouse.

He undressed her slowly, taking in every inch of flawless skin, the gentle curve of her shoulder, the dip at her waist. His body recognized the perfect fit of hers as he stepped into her. He stroked his hand through her hair at the back of her head and fisted her ponytail. "I want you. I want to bury myself inside you and feel your body break apart around mine."

She swallowed hard. "There's something I have to tell you." Her eyes dropped to the floor. "I'm submitting my report Friday."

"I know." The timeline was meticulously detailed in the paperwork and he'd memorized every word, looking for any way out.

"You still want me?" The nervous question struck his heart with a solid thump. She still didn't get it, didn't get him. She had to do what she had to do. He understood because he was in the exact same position. Hopefully, they'd both find a way to heal.

Yanking his t-shirt over his head then shucking his jeans, he held her gaze. "I do, baby. In every way. I want to feast on you and hear my name slip from your sweet lips like a prayer."

Her eyes dilated wide, leaving her irises but a slim ring of green. She stepped into him, burying her face in his neck as he walked them into the shower. As soon as the hot water rained down on their heads, they both tilted their faces to the spray, slicking their hair back.

Then she entwined her arms around his neck. "I want you, too. I forget myself when I'm with you. The world disappears when you touch me."

Her words acted as a salve to his soul even as they cut. The world disappeared, her pain, her worries even, but that didn't mean she was lost in him so much as she was hiding from herself. But he'd take it. How could he expect her to give all of herself when he was in no condition to do the same?

"But first, I want to taste you." Her whisper hit his ears as she pressed her lips to his sternum, then followed the path along the deep ridge of his abs with small, feather-light licks of her tongue.

A low growl vibrated through his chest as she cupped his balls in her slick hands. She slid her hand down to the base of him, then back up and over the head with a firm squeeze and tug. He sucked in a breath, gently kneading her shoulders to keep from demanding more.

The tip of her tongue slid along the tip of him, then her whole mouth wrapped around him and his world went black.

"Jesus Christ," he grated out.

As the hot water pounded down on his torso, she slid up and down the length of him, sucking more of him in then he'd ever thought possible. His thighs tightened against the rising pressure and shook.

"I love the feel of your skin, so soft and so hard at the same time. From the first day you took your shirt off at the well, I wanted to feel you."

148

She gently tugged with her mouth, then swirled her tongue around and around. "You taste so good, Ryker."

"Damn it, woman." He gripped her by the arms and dragged her back up before him. Yanking her to his chest, he lifted her, tucking her legs around his waist. He slammed his mouth onto hers, the shower doing its best to wash away the day, but he could still taste her sweetness.

Kneading deep into the back of her thighs where they met her ass, he lifted and lowered her, sliding her over his length. She tangled her tongue with his, matching the rhythm he set and groaning into his mouth. "I want you. I shouldn't, but I do."

His brain echoed the sentiment but his heart rejected the idea. He didn't want her only to want him, but hungered deep inside for her to need him, to see herself with him to the point that the Cape, the town, nothing else mattered. He wanted her love. But he didn't deserve it.

Leaning back against the tiled wall of the shower, he squeezed his eyes shut to block out the inconvenient direction of his thoughts and just feel.

Her center was wet and slick, different than the water sluicing over them.

"Someday, we're going to have to try this on a bed," she teased.

"Someday." Might never come.

Jerking the shower knob to the off position, he swept her up in his arms and pushed through the door.

"Ryker, what are you doing?"

He padded across the tile to the wood floor then dropped her on the bed. Crawling toward her, he spread her legs as he went. His dick throbbed as her eyes dilated with excitement.

"What are you doing?" she repeated, her question came on a breath.

"I'm loving you, Larkin." He slid his tongue over her, working her with tender caresses. Her hands flew to his head, grabbing fistfuls of hair. The sharp sting to his scalp was a pleasure-pain that shot straight to his dick, and he groaned against her center. His hand slipped up her side to palm her breast, then skim over her rigid nipple.

Her head thrashed back and forth. "Ryker."

"Say you need me." The demand was hollow because he was the one who needed. He needed the words; he needed those closest to him to believe in him.

He slid his body up hers, stopping to lave at her breasts, twirling his tongue around one nipple then the other, and adjusting his body until he was poised to finally feel what he'd wanted since they were leaving their prints on the Cape.

"I need you. Now." Her eyes were closed, her lips parted, lost in the pleasure they found in each other.

Hearing the words shook him to the core, and he flexed his hips, sliding home, connecting them in a way that was deeper than either was prepared for. "Look at me, baby."

She whispered. "Yes, yes."

"Look at me, goddamnit."

Her eyes flew open, wild and unfocused. She found him and locked on. As he sunk deep then pulled back, she gripped his flanks with her thighs, her heels digging into his ass, but she never looked away. "I need you, Ryker. Don't stop."

He increased the pace, his balls drawing tight, his thighs burning and his arms shaking as waves of white hot pleasure rocketed through him. Slamming his mouth to hers, he swallowed her cry of release and met it with his own.

She'd changed him. Made him feel things he'd never allowed himself to believe were possible. His heart split wide open.

He wanted to give her the world, but all she wanted was the Cape.

CHAPTER 16

*L*arkin trailed her hand down the walls of the hallway from her bedroom to the kitchen. Her fingers bumped over the edge of a door frame then fell to the dark wood to rest on the sun's warmth shining through the opposite window. She paused, working through the rush of memories. Early morning snuggles, lullabies and bedtime stories; she could hear the rapid little *thump, thump, thump* of him running down the hall, looking for her.

Archer's room.

Today was the day. Do or die, as they said.

Puzzle weaved his warm little body around her ankles and purred. "Hey there, buddy." She picked up the cat and nuzzled his neck, comforted by his soft warmth.

She wrapped her hand around the knob and turned it.

As the door opened on silent hinges, her heart paused. The sun shone through his window, dust fairies dancing about in the rays. His bed was still covered in his favorite dinosaur and puppy stuffed animals. A picture of her, John, and Archer sat at an angle on his bedside table.

She hadn't been able to change a thing.

It was different with John's belongings. She'd been numb with grief and unable to look at his things without feelings of hate, which shamed her, so she'd packed his things and shipped them off to his mother shortly after the funeral.

But her baby boy's possessions remained exactly the way she'd left them the morning they'd gone to visit Maxine.

How many times had her family and friends encouraged her to go through his room and donate his toys and books? She couldn't begin to count. And her answer was always a swift and solid no.

On particularly lonely nights, like last night after she'd left Ryker, she'd lay in her little boy's bed and let the memories of his smile wash over her. She used to lie with him when he was scared or not feeling well. She'd patiently sit and wait while he struggled to pull on his sweater because he could do it all by himself. Not to mention all the times she'd reorganized his shelves filled with puzzles based on size only to have him reorganize them based on whatever mattered to his little brain.

She moved into the room, letting her fingers trail along the surface of his dresser, his shelves, the foot of his bed, then sunk down to the mattress.

Puzzle crawled from her lap, making himself at home on Archer's pillow.

Her chest was heavy and she tried to pull air in past the constriction in her throat. The pain never seemed easier, only more and more familiar.

Last night had been particularly difficult. When she'd left Ryker, they were both in a weird and somber mood. It was as if they both dreaded facing the night alone but had no choice. She couldn't stay and he didn't ask her.

His demand for her to say she needed him had torn at her heart. Not only for the pain she recognized in his, but for the pain the admission would bring to her own. Needing him made what she had to do all the more difficult. Wanting him was fine, desiring him was natural, needing him and still going after his home was impossible. The constant guilt of fighting him for what was rightfully his exhausted her and tore at her in a way she'd never considered.

But she hadn't considered she'd ever fall in love either.

Archer's lighthouse puzzle from Maxine caught her eye and she scooted from the bed to sit cross-legged on the floor. Pulling the box down from a shelf, she studied the front cover then dumped the pieces in front of her.

Piece by piece, she established the border. The day Maxine had given him the gift, he'd hollered in delight and zoomed around the grounds like an airplane before finally settling in his surrogate grandmother's lap to get to work.

"Today's the day, Archer. I'm going to the courthouse to meet the Judge save the Cape," she whispered.

Silence rang in her ears as she continued to piece the puzzle together. As she snapped the final shape into place, a light wash of goosebumps lit across her shoulders. She peered closer at the final picture.

It had been taken from the well, and up in the middle window was Archer with his hand in the air, waving. She could just barely see his features under his shock of blond hair, his sparkling eyes and his mischievous grin.

She was doing the right thing. The Cape was bigger than her pain, bigger than Ryker's. It held the potential of helping the whole community. And she had to save it since she couldn't save her son.

"Okay," she whispered.

Seagulls squawked outside, pulling her attention to Archer's window. The front of her house faced the North Cove. Just down the road from The Hideaway and Stay Inn, she was one of only a few houses along the shore.

The lighthouse was visible off in the distance. Archer loved to watch it when Mr. Stull would test the lamp. She followed the curve of the Cape until her eyes rested on the large Victorian house, but then the open space closed up with the north edge of woods that created one side of a horseshoe of trees that covered the Cape going toward town.

She couldn't see the well, and for a moment, a streak of fear sliced through her chest. Rolling her shoulders back, she tried to shake it off. Nothing was going to happen to the well; nothing was going to happen to the Cape.

She'd see to it.

Pushing up from the floor, she brushed at her suit then buttoned her jacket. Her computer with her presentation was ready to go on the dining table, her printouts of pertinent information outlining the endangered species found, the rare plants, everything that proved the Cape should be preserved.

The time was now...because never was *not* an option.

On the way to town, she focused on the sun shining in a pattern of speckles through the trees and thought of the victory dinner she'd planned with her mom and dad at Delizioso's. She could already taste their homemade tiramisu.

As she made her way across the courthouse parking lot, the top of the large pine tree by the town library shook gently. She could only guess at how many children were hiding up in that thing, laughter and screams riding on the breeze from the playground on the other side.

Over in the square, the slate-colored canopy of the Fountain of Youth center stage hid the spraying water that was splashing in the comforting and constant rhythm familiar to anyone from Cape Van Buren. If there was ever a sign of potential, it was the Fountain of Youth. Legend had it that explorers had scoured the Northeast coast, searching for the magical healing waters found there.

She grinned, her heart bursting with possibility.

She loved this town. She loved the coastal, old-world feel of the weathered brick buildings, wrought iron, rope, and wood. She loved seeing the ocean from different points in town, the Cape's lighthouse from others, and the Fountain of Youth from just about anywhere.

It was all connected. *They* were all connected and her plans for the Cape would only continue to foster that beautiful, unified link between the town and the people.

The courthouse had the hushed vibration of a church, leaving her nerves thrumming and her self-confidence a bit shaky.

"Ms. Sinclair? Judge Carter's ready for you."

Larkin followed the young woman into the judge's chambers, immediately put on guard by the way Judge Carter's brows pulled together as she walked in. Pulling from every ounce of faith in her heart, she lifted her chin and gave him her brightest smile.

"Good afternoon, Judge Carter." She reached her hand across his desk to shake his hand.

"Please, sit down, Larkin. You know you don't have to be so formal with me. Maxine's going to have my ass as it is without making you follow all the pomp and circumstance of the courthouse. You should have met me at DEP."

Dread pooled in her stomach as she stared at the judge. He wouldn't quite meet her eyes, but shifted his gaze about his desk and office.

"I'm not getting it, am I?" Her stomach twisted.

He grabbed a stack of papers from his desk, tapping them straight then setting them back down. "Ryker has a sharp team. Not only did they come in with some additional rather brilliant ideas on preserving some of the most protected attributes of the estate, such as the bee colony, but they also found a bylaw that actually grandfathers the Cape from ever being handed over to the state."

A low buzzing grew in her head and she lowered to the tufted leather chair. Her fingers went numb, breathing hurt her chest. She gave her head a small shake. "When?" She was just with Ryker a few days earlier, had told him she was submitting her work. He never let on about his findings.

And why would he? Business was his priority. He had the same rights she did to fight for the Cape. He'd just done it better. Hell, he had a team of experts for this exact reason.

All the work she'd done had been for nothing. Pain squeezed through her body and a lump rose in her throat.

She'd promised to save the Cape for Archer but once again she was powerless to save what she loved. What he'd loved.

Thanking the judge, she hurried from the courthouse to her car, fighting for composure.

It couldn't be over. There had to be something she could do.

She needed to talk to Ryker, tell him her plans. Maybe if she laid out her whole vision, he could see what she was trying to do. What they could do together.

Because now that she was hurting, he was who she was running to. He was who she wanted to see, who she wanted to share her pain and disappointment with. Somehow, he'd become her lighthouse, her safety in the storm. She loved him and they made a formidable team.

She had to believe he felt the same.

~

Slamming her brakes hard, Larkin skidded to a stop in the roundabout in front of the house. Construction trucks were everywhere with the crews already staking out boundary lines and marker flags for water and electricity.

She searched the men for the one who could turn this day around, who could make it all right. Ryker's dark head was bent over a large land map just as it was that fateful day she'd learned of his plans. Exiting her car, she threw the door shut then ran toward him. Once she hit the grass, her heels sunk into the soft earth so she ditched her shoes and closed the distance in her bare feet.

"Ryker!"

He looked up then glanced at his men, saying something. They nodded and stepped away.

His eyes skimmed over her, settling on her face. "You heard the news."

She swallowed hard at the site of the large backhoe a few yards from the well. A large orange X was painted on the bottom of a neighboring tree.

Archer used to climb that tree.

"Please. Wait. Can we talk? If I can explain my plan…" She shoved her hands out, palms up to prove she wasn't hiding anything.

A flash of regret shone from his eyes but he slowly shook his head, his brows furrowed. "I don't think you should be out here right now. I know this is hard."

"Did you know? When I was here? Is that where your show of affection came from? Your guilt?" Her tone rose in accusation.

"Don't do that. We both accepted from the beginning that we had to do what we had to do. You were trying to make the Cape your own. But it was already mine."

"No." She cut her hand through the air. "Not my own. The town's. I want to preserve the beauty that is here, use the Cape to educate and unite the people more than ever before. Allow people to really live, to really experience what this place has to offer."

His gaze darkened, like billowing clouds blotting out the moon. Treading lightly was paramount. He'd suffered deeply as a child, but the Cape wasn't the cause, his horrible father had been. Her eyes darted to the well and back. She couldn't lose the Cape. She couldn't lose the only connection she had with her little boy. Tears pushed at her lids as panic clawed its way up her throat.

Ryker looked at her with eyes full of pity as she gripped her hands at her sides against the pain of it all. "Larkin, you've barely begun living yourself. How do you think you can inspire others to do so?"

She flinched at his words, taken aback by the bluntness of it all.

"You're holding on to memories, holding on to the past, instead of living and moving forward."

Maxine's car pulled up, and she and Blayne got out, hurrying toward them. Larkin barely spared them a glance. News traveled fast in Cape Van Buren.

She held his dark gaze, as painful as it was.

The backhoe beeped a back-up warning and she glanced at it, distracted as she spoke. "That's rich, coming from you." Pain squeezed her chest. "I might be living in my past, but you refuse to deal with yours. You're bent on destroying everything that was good about it because you are so tightly holding onto your anger."

The backhoe continued to move, inching closer to the well. Surely, they'd see they were getting too close.

Ryker responded but she didn't hear him.

The backhoe wasn't stopping.

"Ryker." She tried to get him to stop talking, to shut up about strength and intent, but all she could focus on was the awful beeping and the distance closing between the backhoe and the well.

"Ryker, wait! Please, listen to me." She stepped closer, trying to get his attention, but he was ticking items off his fingers, not realizing what was happening right behind his back.

Both Maxine and Blayne hurried forward, and his grandmother called out, "Ryker stop them."

"Ryker!" Larkin yelled, and she grabbed him by the arms, giving him a shove just as the backhoe jerked back once again, crashing into the stone, making a sickening sound of brick raining down into the water below.

Ryker spun around.

Larkin fell to her knees on a cry. Every memory of Archer rushing through her mind like a flash flood of wishes and laughter, bright hazel eyes and dimpled grins.

It was over.

It was all over.

The well was destroyed, the Cape was Ryker's, her boy was dead. Every crushing reality crashed over her like the rocks to the bottom of the well.

She tried to pull in a breath but her lungs burned and refused to open. Blayne dropped beside her, pulling Larkin into her chest. "It's going to be okay."

Ryker turned back, his face ashen, and hurried to Larkin's side. "I didn't know."

He reached for her but she jerked back, stumbling to her feet.

"No. Don't *touch* me." Her voice was shaking but clear. "You destroy everything you touch. You've destroyed everything that could be good, that would be good for you, for me, because you're bent on avenging the little boy who grew up here with so much pain and terror." She swiped at the tears streaming down her cheeks. "But you missed the idea that it may have already been avenged. That balance had been restored through the joy and love and power that another little boy did experience here." She spoke through her tears, her voice thick, her throat burning.

She backed away from the ruin of the well, the destruction of her memories. She backed away from Ryker, she backed away from Maxine, and even Blayne. Shaking her head, she swallowed hard. "It was never the Cape, but your father who was to blame. You just refused to see it because deep down you're still afraid of him."

She moved away from the crowd. The urgency to hide, to be as far away from everyone as possible, was strong but she could barely breathe, barely think.

"Larkin, wait. Please, don't go."

She paused, looking over her shoulder. Ryker stood with one foot stepping forward as if wanting to go to her, but afraid to touch her again.

She turned away. "There's nothing left for me here."

Blinded by tears, she made her way to her car. Tugging on the door, she dropped her keys with a curse as Blayne stepped beside her, carrying her shoes. "You can't drive."

"No one is ever going to tell me what I can and can't do again."

Blayne flinched but picked up the keys nonetheless. "Get in the car. You're in no condition to drive."

But Larkin was frozen. She couldn't step forward, couldn't step back.

Blayne's arms came around her and she gently guided her to the passenger side of the car. She sat and the door closed, leaving her in a silent vacuum of despair.

The absoluteness of her new reality slammed like the bricks of the well against her chest.

She'd failed.

She'd failed her son, not once but twice. She'd failed the town. She failed the animals and plants that could only find home on the cape.

Blinking through her tears, she heard the echo of the awful things she'd said to Ryker.

She'd failed the little boy who lived within him, too, because she hadn't reached him, hadn't been able to make him see.

The Cape would be gone.

The well was gone.

In a panic, she lowered her window and concentrated hard to hear Archer's voice through the treetops or his laughter on the wind chimes.

Silence.

And that was most excruciating of all.

Archer was gone, too.

~

"What have you done?" Maxine whispered, looking at the crushed well with a look of horror.

A heavy band of regret and self-recrimination tightened in Ryker's chest, and a low, steady pounding rocked through his head. The well was never supposed to have been touched. It was going to be a focal point of the community. He'd even planned to have it dedicated to Archer as a special gift to Larkin.

The look on her face had crushed him in a way that stole his breath and slayed his soul.

He blinked at his grandmother, trying to pull himself together.

The driver of the backhoe kicked a few bricks out of the rubble.

Out of nowhere, Ryker roared, "LEAVE IT!" surprising everyone, including himself.

The driver lifted his hands in front of his chest in a sign of surrender and slinked away.

Ryker circled the well, stepping over broken bricks and mortar. The peaked wooden roof lay in pieces with a rope hanging limply from one rod. The bucket was nowhere in sight. The flowers that circled the base lay crushed beneath the bricks. It was destroyed.

Rubbing a hand over his face, he studied the rubble. It wasn't supposed to end like this. He'd had a plan. A plan that would have righted all the wrongs, that would have brought beauty and opportunity to the whole town of Cape Van Buren.

He was a fool for letting himself get so close to Larkin. Not only because of the untenable situation between them, but because they both had wounds that ran too deep, too raw. He wasn't good for her, and she wasn't good for him.

She made him want things that his heart didn't have the capacity to withstand.

And once he was good and well sold on the idea that just maybe they could have a future together, she crushed the dream with one inarguable declaration. *"There's nothing left for me here."*

He wasn't enough.

He'd never been enough.

"Ryker."

He shook his head. "Leave it, Grandmother."

A shape on one of the bricks caught his eye. Squatting down, ignoring the ache in his knees and the pain in his heart, he moved sections of brick and mortar until he got a clear view.

There amongst the rubble were Archer's small hand prints.

Broken into pieces.

CHAPTER 17

$\mathcal{L}$arkin stepped carefully across the grass of the cemetery, counting the birch trees that ran along one side until she stood at Archer's gravestone. She didn't need to count the trees but it had become a centering exercise for her since the day they'd buried her little boy. It gave her time to focus on her breaths. Time she needed before seeing his name etched in granite.

But as she stared at the scripted line that made the first stroke of the letter A, she forgot how to breathe again. She blinked a few times, surprised by how much the action burned her lungs. His name lay at her feet, the stone proof that he'd existed, but she didn't feel him. Not here. Something Ryker couldn't understand. Or wouldn't.

Days had passed since the well had been crushed into rubble but the vision had played an excruciating loop in her head ever since. By now, Ryker probably had all the lots staked out and foundations poured. There was no telling if he planned to leave the lighthouse. It would be a shame to see the beautiful building torn down but she wouldn't put it past him. His only focus was destruction.

She sank to the soft grass. The reality of failing Archer filled her chest, crowding her lungs. She wanted to rail and scream and pound her fists in the earth, but she'd made noise and now the Cape was lost. It was probably better if the universe didn't notice her at all.

She'd tried to live, tried to find a purpose, but in the end she'd only made things worse. A teasing glimpse of the life she'd let herself dream of on the Cape with Ryker mocked her, and a tear slipped down her cheek.

She cried for Archer, for herself, for a little plot of land that had brought them such joy. How could Maxine have sold it to a man who didn't cherish it, didn't love it?

She ached for him, for the beautiful, profoundly broken man she'd foolishly fallen in love with, but she also simply ached.

The sun had long since passed the highest point in the sky and had begun its descent to the west. But she continued to sit in her frozen state of panic. She couldn't face going home, seeing Archer's empty room, or the lighthouse puzzle still on the floor where she'd left it. She couldn't go back to the Cape.

She was stuck in a place where she had to leave but didn't know where to go.

"I thought I might find you here."

Larkin swiped at her tears, blinking a few times, and pushed up onto her knees.

Claire lowered next to her, mirroring her position. "I used to see you here all the time those first few months. Sitting here with Archer." She pointed down the hill toward the little duck pond behind them. "My fiancé is buried just past that cluster of trees on the other side of the water." Sitting back, she pulled her legs around, bending them at the knees and wrapping her arms around them.

"I used to hate you for having your son, for having had your husband. And then I noticed you never visited John's grave." Claire stood up and put a hand out. "Come."

Larkin stared at the offered hand in surprise but accepted the help up to her feet.

"Where are we going?"

"There's a reason you don't visit John's grave. Take me to it," Claire demanded.

Larkin stopped in her tracks. "No."

Claire pinned her with thoughtful blue eyes. "All this time, I thought I had it worse than you. You had memories with your son, birthdays, holidays, and anniversaries with your husband. But he took that all away from you. Well, him and my fiancé." She pulled her shoulders back with the last sentence.

"I don't want to talk about this." Placing a kiss to the palm of her own hand, Larkin held it out toward Archer's grave then turned toward her car.

"Take me to him, Larkin. I've never asked you for anything, but you've continued to ask of me."

Nothing could have been more direct. She spun around. "I wanted to help you." She shoved the hair that had fallen from her ponytail back off her face. "We've been avoiding each other for the past two years."

"And now I'm helping you. That's the whole point of your little plan, isn't it?"

The numb, cold weight that accompanied thoughts of John filled her chest. She looked back toward her car. She could be home and back in her bed in twenty minutes.

"Larkin." Claire grabbed her hand.

On a sigh, she walked down the hill a ways. "He's buried next to his father. Over here." She pointed to two flat stones side by side.

"You're angry," Claire whispered.

She shook her head but the action was a lie. And she was tired of carrying it with her. "Yes. I'm furious. I hate him." She looked at his headstone then back at Claire. "He killed my son. Maybe your fiancé, too. We'll never really know. Do you know how many times I warned him of his temper when he was driving? How many times he brushed it off and told me I was being naive?" She squeezed her eyes shut against the rush of anger.

"Tell him."

Blinking, she cocked her head at Claire. Tell him? She should have made more of an effort to tell him when it would have mattered, when it could have stopped him from putting Archer in danger.

"Tell him, Larkin. I've done my yelling. I've railed at my fiancé for stealing our future, for taking my dreams. Your husband didn't kill him. The investigation proved he was as fully committed as your husband, neither applying the brakes until it was too late."

She rubbed Larkin's arm. "Tell him."

She was a fool to consider such a thing, but as she stared at his name so perfectly engraved on the stone with the words 'beloved father,' something snapped.

Her chest filled with a heavy burn and she swallowed back the tears that threatened. He didn't deserve the honor.

"You did this," she said with a shake in her voice. Pointing at the stone, she stared hard at his name. "You killed our son. Your stupid pride, your stupid temper. I hate you for it, John. I hate you for killing my little boy." She was yelling at this point. Shocked by the sound, she sniffed abruptly. Tears streamed down her face and she clamped her lips closed.

They weren't for her husband. They were for her. For the pain of living without her son.

With a catch in her breath, she added. "And I hate myself for not stopping you." She dropped her face in her hands and let go. For Archer, the Cape, the mistakes of her husband, the weakness within herself. For every moment she wished she could go back and do just one thing differently.

One thing.

The tension in her shoulders eased just a bit, the tight band around her chest loosening.

Claire put her arms around her. "It's not your fault," she whispered, smoothing the hair from Larkin's temples. "And I was unfair for ever making you feel like somehow it was."

Larkin stepped back, needing to stand on her own two feet. "No, you didn't, you—

"Yes, I did. And at first, it felt good. Then I felt like a bully, but my own pain hurt too much when it was just mine. Misery loves company." She held Larkin's gaze. "But you came after me anyway, determined to be friends whether I wanted it or not. I've also found friends in Maxine and Blayne. The Mavens never let me pass without committing to coffee or to help in the garden." She laughed. "I can't be alone now even when I want to be."

With a shrug, Claire looked around the cemetery. "You did that. So I needed to do this for you. After you first approached me to talk, I started seeing a therapist. She's helped a lot and made me face my own buried emotions. It's a journey, but I've started. It's time you did the same."

Walking back toward their cars, weaving in and out of tombstones, trying not to step directly over where a body lay beneath, Larkin glanced at Claire. She'd turned out to be such a surprise. Losing the Cape didn't just affect herself, their whole plan was now on hold. She'd failed more than Archer. If she didn't continue to try, she'd be failing Claire, too. And the community.

That was unacceptable.

"We don't have the Cape but that doesn't mean we still can't continue planning our outreach. We can add to this community in ways no one else can. We have a different perspective, you and I. We dream of everything we would have done for our babies, and that is what we'll do for Cape Van Buren," she said, twisting her hands at her waist as all the possibilities revealed themselves one by one.

Claire leaned against the driver's side door of her car, nodding encouragingly, bolstering Larkin's spirits with her quiet strength.

"I wasn't able to conserve the Cape but it will still be there." She closed her eyes as an image of the ruined well popped into her head. "If Ryker keeps the main house, maybe we can rent space for our outreach, at least until it grows beyond the walls of the place."

Claire smiled. "You really want to do this?"

"I need to." Larkin hugged her. "Thank you."

"Thank *you*."

As Larkin pulled out from Van Buren Cemetery, she circled Van Buren Square and made a list of all the viable locations for the new outreach center, just in case. The whole point of her project was to make services available to the community that would enhance every life. Some might find that help through art classes, some through bereavement groups, some from learning about the natural habitat they were so blessed to call home.

The fact was, there were many different ways for people to heal and to grow.

Some folks needed the chance to start fresh. She frowned. That's what Ryker had needed.

But she'd been so intent on guaranteeing her own needs that she'd been willing to justify why he should deal with his pain on her terms. She hadn't been fair. Maybe if she had been stronger, she could have worked with him instead of against him.

They'd already proven what a great team they could be. Why hadn't she seen it?

All she needed to heal had been within her the whole time.

As she got out of her car, a tinkling melody came from the backyard. She rounded the corner of the house until she had a clear view of Archer's wind chimes hanging from a pine tree in the yard. Her heart squeezed and she smiled.

He wasn't only at the well; he was within her, always was and always would be.

He was in her memories, in her stories, in the way she cared about people, and the way she'd continue to care about people.

Looking out across the choppy waves of the North Cove, she could just make out figures moving about the property. But what held her attention were the glowing rays from the lighthouse. Ryker had turned it on. There'd be no reason to do so if he was going to tear it all down.

A small kernel of hope bloomed in her chest. If she could just keep her view of the lighthouse...it was funny how her brain grabbed onto every possible tether.

Like the possibility of love.

If she were honest, she'd fallen in love with Ryker the moment he'd shoved a plate with two cupcakes in front of her on the morning she'd come to his house with the stay on the property. And again when he held her gaze as she told stories about her son, and when he held her as she cried, and every time he challenged her views and accepted her values.

Her heart dropped.

She'd said awful things to him, unfair things. But she'd been hurting and panicked when she failed to win the conservation. By the time the backhoe was backing toward the well, she had reached her breaking point and couldn't see past her own heartache.

Making her way back around the house, she sighed. She'd accused him of still being afraid of his father, of not standing up to him as an adult, when she'd been guilty of the same thing with her husband.

Even worse.

She should have been standing up for Archer.

In the end, she and Ryker weren't meant to be together. Too much pain separated them in a way an ocean of water never could.

But thanks to him, she'd loved again. And that was living, even if losing it caused such awful pain.

Archer would be proud.

∼

*M*itch headed toward Ryker's front door. "Starting the project late is worse than the stay on the property, man. You need to pull your shit together."

If only he knew how. He missed Larkin so much he felt like he was going mad. Five days. Five long days had passed since the woman he loved collapsed to the ground because he was a complete and utter ass.

He believed in his plans for the Cape, but losing focus on-site and not stopping the backhoe was unforgivable. And now he hadn't been able to stomach having his crew on the property. They were all holed up at South Cove Bungalow, waiting to start.

He grabbed his bee suit as he showed his buddy the front door. "I'm getting really tired of pandering to their egos, to be honest. Maybe Van Buren Enterprises needs to be the sole entity funding this project."

Mitch spun around on the front porch. "You can't be serious. One thing goes wrong and you'll be ruined. You need to think about this, Ryker."

"Don't question my business sense." He spoke in a low tone that brooked no argument and narrowed his gaze in a way that had his crew in New York stepping back.

But the middle finger his buddy gave him demonstrated the fucker couldn't care less. "Don't be a dick. I'll question you all the hell I want. You're being a jackass. And jackasses make bad decisions." He jerked his thumb over his shoulder toward the lighthouse. "Hell, you're making the damn lamp operational before you have a means of paying for it."

Ryker moved past him and down the steps. He had to light the lamp. After what he let happen with the well, he hadn't been able to sleep, couldn't concentrate. One night, he'd climbed the stairs he'd once taken with Larkin until he found himself cleaning the windows and wiping down the lens. Remembering the first sensation of her lips against his, the soft weight of her against his chest as he carried her down the stairs, and her look of utter hilarity at the whole situation once she was safely grounded with no bees around.

Then he lit it.

Larkin would be able to see it from her house and, for some reason, the knowledge let him sleep finally. It killed him not to see her, not to go to her, but all he brought her was pain. It was time he thought of someone other than himself. So he'd stayed away.

Jerking his chin toward the drive, he ground out, "You can see your way out."

Mitch studied him. "You know, you need to figure your shit out and soon. What the hell do you want? Do you even know anymore?" He walked backward toward his truck. "Let me know if Maxine needs any more help getting her things from the attic."

"*I'll* help my grandmother."

"Yeah? Well, when are you going to let her help you? 'Cause I don't think you really want to go through with your plan anymore. You're just too damn stubborn to see it. You don't have to be afraid. Your dad's no longer a threat. You know this."

Ryker shook his head. "I'm not afraid."

But Mitch wasn't listening. He slid behind the wheel and gunned his engine.

Like he had any room to talk about life decisions or being afraid. The guy ran through women like flatlanders did lobster tails. The only thing he'd ever committed to was his job, and even that was solely dependent on him as an independent attorney. He had no firm, no one to report to.

Ryker sighed and let his head fall back as his buddy's truck disappeared down the drive. What he needed now was a bit of peace. He needed to go work with his bees.

Approaching the hives on the north side of the Cape rather than where he'd run his hands down Larkin's naked body, he slid on his hood. The bees would help center him, allow him to make a plan and get his project back on track.

Because Mitch didn't know what he was talking about.

He rubbed his chest as he took in the activity of the super. The hum coming from the bees grew louder. Sliding the lid to the side, he gave a quick inspection to the honey frames. There was a bit of burr comb build-up to take care of but the bees were all over the place.

Grabbing a brush, he gently moved a few from the top, only increasing their irritation. A bit of smoke didn't work either. What the fuck was wrong with him today?

Suddenly a burning sensation in the middle of his back made him drop the smoker and spin around. Goddamn bastard stung him through this suit while the fabric had pulled tight. The buzz grew louder and no amount of deep breathing was calming him or the bees down.

His one place of peace was turning against him. He slid the lid back in place then grabbed his tools, ignoring the lie he told himself and the pinpoint of fire on his back.

Beekeeping wasn't his only peace.

Larkin grounded him like no one ever had before. He was centered with her. And he'd never say the words out loud but she made him feel safe. Swallowing the derisive chuckle that attempted to bubble up his throat, he made his way across the grounds toward the house just as his grandmother pulled up.

As she got out of her car, he called to her. "I really need to get a lock on that gate."

"Pfft! I'd just climb over it," Maxine said.

And he believed it, too.

"Besides, you'll have your locked gate for your high-end community homes anytime now, won't you?"

Hearing the words left a hollow feeling in his gut and fucked with the validity of his plans. The community would be thriving with opportunities for beekeeping, utilization of the lighthouse, events at Van Buren House. His well-defined, environmentally-sound, and equitably smart plan was the main reason the courts granted him his rights back. The grandfather clause Mitch had found was only if he'd needed backup.

But the more time he'd spent with Larkin, the more important it became that he did right by the property. Even if it wouldn't be his home anymore.

Anymore.

Was it ever, really?

His grandmother kissed his cheek, the scent of her perfume wrapping around his head, making him think of cookies and scavenger hunts. She'd always made him laugh, made every moment with her special.

She smoothed down her royal blue silk shirt, silver bracelets dangling from her wrists. "What's going on? Teddy told me you hadn't put your crew to work yet."

He loved the way her silver hair caught the sun. It shone every bit as much as her jewelry.

"Grandmother, why didn't you and Grandfather leave me the Cape?"

Her smile faltered a bit as she took his hand. They walked along the south shore, where a piece of land spread into a small sandbar, then along the sharp rocks jutting out to the sea.

"Where's this coming from?" she asked.

"When James was out here, he said something about if I was so special, so worthy, why didn't Grandfather leave me the Cape? Why'd I have to buy it? And to be clear, I don't mind a single cent I spent. I'm just trying to figure some shit out."

She sighed. "I've tried to protect you, though most of the time, I've felt completely helpless."

"I know. But I couldn't tell the police. I didn't trust James not to carry out his threats, and if he'd have ever hurt you, I'd have killed him."

She reached out and cupped his face. "But it was my job to protect you."

"You did. As much as I'd let you."

The waves in the South Cove were choppy, their little white caps riding each wave as it crashed into the rocks below them. Maxine focused on them a moment, then held his gaze once again.

"Well, one way I was able to protect you was by keeping your parents from using you as an adult. Your dad gambled and lost big, then your mother was asking for your contact information in New York, but I'd heard from my girlfriend Marge down in Florida that your mother was looking to buy a house. I couldn't stand the thought of her asking you for anything. I didn't want any of it to touch you. So I used what was left of my inheritance from my parents and refinanced the estate and sent her the money."

The world seemed to tilt then right itself.

"I know the Cape brings terrible memories for you, sweetheart, but it brings a lifetime of beautiful ones to me, and the most precious was the day you were brought home from the hospital. I just knew you'd be my little shadow from day one. Your big brown eyes locked on mine like we'd already met."

Tears welled above her lower lashes but she blinked them back. "You were always supposed to get the Cape. It was always for you. Grandfather wanted it more than anything, but we no longer owned it outright and I had to sell it in order to move."

She stepped in front of him and he stopped walking. "You are our pride, our love, our joy. You've always been enough. Been worthy. You have to stop letting your father's hurtful words affect you. He's damaged and can't seem to stop himself from trying to destroy the only good thing he's done in his life."

She grabbed his hand and held it to her heart. "But it's time for you to move on, my sweet. Your father may not have appreciated you, but you mean the absolute world to me and to your grandfather. And this land—" She waved her arm out, rings sparkling in the afternoon sun "—is where we made our very best memories with you. The lighthouse, the bees, our scavenger hunts, and you always sneaking around when I had the Mavens over for our late-night moonshine."

He chuckled. "You knew?"

"I did." She nodded. "But I knew we made you feel safe."

He dipped his chin. "I don't know what I'm doing anymore, Grandmother." Fool didn't even begin to explain how he felt. He was three times the woman's size but when he was with her it was as if he was the scared little boy or the angry teenager.

"You love her. I knew you would." She placed her hand over his heart.

He frowned. "I ruined everything. But even if I hadn't, she's stuck in her past. I understand it but I can never compete with it. Besides, it's not like I've got my shit together either. I don't want to hurt her any more than I already have."

Maxine put her hands on her hips. "Bullshit."

He raised a brow with a chuckle. "Excuse me?"

"You heard me. When are all the excuses going to stop? She may be living in her past, but you're running from yours. When both of you should wake the hell up and see the beautiful gift that is right in front of you...right now."

But the truth was, as much as he didn't want to hurt Larkin, he didn't want to be hurt. He was tired of running from his pain only to find more. When she told him there was nothing left for her on the Cape, it was if she'd sliced him in half. He wasn't enough to make her stay.

Walking alongside his grandmother, he imagined his community thriving. Children running between houses, cars in the driveways, maybe couples fishing along the north shore. But something kept snagging.

It would be too crowded. You'd never really see the children running or anyone fishing because the rows of houses would block the view. As it was, his plan required thinning of the trees and relocation of the beehives.

They rounded the rubble of the well and Maxine averted her gaze.

"I never meant for that to happen."

She grabbed his hand and patted it. "I know you didn't. Listen, I'm meeting Teddy at Van Buren Boat Club to take the boat out. Thank you for the work you did. Grandfather's boat is gleaming."

He dipped his chin. "Happy to help."

"I'm glad you're home, however long that may be."

He stood staring down the drive long after her car disappeared into the trees. He struggled with the peace that filled his chest at her words. But there was still a hole burning in his gut.

No, that wasn't right, not still, but rather a new one. Left by a certain green-eyed temptress with her honey locks and silky skin.

He kicked a piece of brick, and it skipped along the top of the pile, rolling to a stop next to the sections of Archer's handprints. He stared at the indention hard as he rounded the pile.

Life was a puzzle. He finally found the woman who made him feel whole and good and worthy, but he'd wanted her to leave her past and join him in the future, not appreciating how excruciating the journey could be. How could he expect her to relinquish all her pain and move on with him when he had such difficulty doing the same?

What he did know was that he could no longer imagine moving forward without her.

Squatting next to the brick, he carefully moved the pieces around until he'd collected all of Archer's hand prints.

An idea flickered and grew bright like the glow from Cape Van Buren's lighthouse.

The answer to life's puzzle was simple.

Now he just had to hope Larkin could see it.

CHAPTER 18

A few days had floated by, leaving Larkin with a bit of clarity and a lot of resolve. She had to apologize to Ryker and let go of the Cape once and for all. It had been all she could hold on to until she was ready to hold on to herself.

She was finally ready.

Time to reboot and make plans with Claire and Blayne for the outreach. But first, she'd apologize and drop off her freshly baked blueberry pie. She lifted her chin a notch as she drove over the bridge, then turned onto North Cove Ave. toward town. There would always be reminders of Archer all around Cape Van Buren that were both good and bad. Being able to handle each one was part of moving forward, and it was time she upheld her promise to her little boy. It was time to start living again.

As she approached the entrance gate to the Cape, she slowed down for the turn and braced herself. Facing the man she loved and letting him go wasn't any easier than releasing the Cape itself. Not seeing his intense dark gaze or feeling the strength of his broad hands would be torture. One she'd have to work on being able to endure.

She glanced up at the sign, ready to see the familiar letters that spelled out *Cape Van Buren est. 1879,* and hit the brakes. Dirt and gravel flew up around the front of her car, leaving a cloud of dust floating toward the sun.

She stared at the words, a wash of emotion overwhelming her breath. Her heart slammed hard and fast against her ribs as she pushed open the car door and slid from the seat. Her mind couldn't make sense of what she was reading.

The Archer Conservation Park of Cape Van Buren

~ the answer to life's puzzle is love ~

Her heart squeezed and her fingers flew to her locket as she tried to reconcile the sign with the reality of the week. Then she looked closer. Below the words were hand prints. Ryker's prints were the base, with her prints within his, and then...tears welled, spilling onto her cheeks, and she pulled in a shaky breath.

Inside her prints were Archer's, pieced together like the puzzles he loved so much.

She covered her mouth with a shaky hand and tried to swallow.

Beneath the sign, the gate opened slow and steady with its accompanying squeak and groan, revealing Ryker, Blayne, Claire, Maxine, Mitch, and her parents.

"Daddy?" she called out, confused. He waved, sporting the steady grin she grew up counting on.

They all walked toward her, love shining from their eyes, and something else.

Something that looked a lot like hope.

"I don't understand," she said shaking her head and pointing at her son's name in the large sign.

Ryker stood before her, his dark eyes holding hers with determination. Her heart soared at the sight of him, as if it was finally able to pump again. He looked bigger, broader, and more ruggedly handsome than ever. She blinked to clear her head and steady her resolve.

"I'm sorry," he said, reaching for her then letting his hand drop to his side.

"No. I am. I was coming to apologize. I brought you pie." She finished weakly.

His lips pulled up at the corners, shifting the scruff that covered his jaw. She wanted to run her fingers over it to feel the stubble against her skin. She wanted him to hold her and make all the pain go away.

"You and your gifts." He studied her. "This time you're delivering it instead of your signature drop and dash?"

Heat rose in her cheeks. She'd been hiding from herself, from life for so long; she hadn't noticed just how much she'd been avoiding real moments.

He cleared his throat and it sounded like gravel falling over itself. "I'm the one who needs to apologize. I was stubborn and closed-minded and in the end, reckless. I never meant for the well to be damaged. I was so blinded by my own baggage that I couldn't see beyond it. I couldn't see you. Not the way I can now."

She swallowed hard past all the words that came rushing out. "I was no better. I pushed and pushed for you to see things my way to save the memories of my little boy." Looking around at her family and friends, she closed her eyes then found his again. "When you were trying to heal the memories of the little boy you used to be." She smiled with a small shake of her head. "I didn't see you either."

He clasped her hands and she stared at how easily hers disappeared. Her heart settled in her chest. She was home.

This was living.

Ryker, her friends, her family. She didn't need the Cape, she just needed them. Archer was reflected in each and every one of their gazes.

She swallowed hard, afraid to look away, afraid to breathe.

"I'm so sorry for the awful things I said to you. They were unforgivable and unkind," she said brokenly.

He slid his hands up her arms, pulling her closer to him. "As hard as it was to hear, I needed to hear it. A wake-up call to quit living in the past. I wish it wouldn't have taken the destruction of the well to make me listen. No apology can fix that but I want to try."

She sunk into his chest, taking comfort in his masculine scent. "So you forgive me then?"

A soft chuckle rumbled against her cheek. "I think we've easily established that it's you who I hope will forgive me."

All their pain and fears and worries seemed to float about them, waiting to be empowered or rendered useless through a sweeping release.

It was time to let go.

Time to move ahead.

And time to forgive.

"I do."

Every muscle in his body tensed against her and he leaned back to look into her eyes. "You do?" Yearning shone from his like a wavering olive branch.

She nodded not trusting herself to speak.

"You and I make a great team. Over these past few weeks we've proven that time and again." With a gentle finger, he lifted her chin. "I'm not developing the Cape, cupcake."

She froze, hope and disbelief constricting her throat.

"What do you mean?" she whispered. "What about the community? Your plans?"

"I found a better one. Someone once told me that this land held a multitude of rare animals and plants. Then Claire and Blayne filled me in on your plans for the outreach community center. I figured my best investment would be in us. You and me. The Cape. This town."

He turned her to face the sign. "I'm taking advantage of a conservation easement."

Her heart fluttered in her chest like a butterfly with new wings.

"I can live on the estate while preserving the plants and wildlife."

She ran her gaze over his face. His eyes were intense with possibility, his brows furrowed with intent.

He reached for her. "We can work out a business plan for the community center, something that really reflects all the lessons Archer taught us."

Her lips trembled on a smile and she took his hand

"Remember I told you my grandfather used to tell me to be silent to hear true wisdom? I finally listened. The true value of my future isn't the money I make or destroying my memories, but having you by my side. We haven't known each other long. But I know you're mine, cupcake. And I'm yours. We can take as long as you need, but tell me you'll stay," he demanded. Then cleared his throat. "Please."

She looked at the hopeful faces of her parents, Maxine, and the girls. Even Mitch was hanging on every word, which made her smile. "You all knew about this?"

She couldn't believe any of this was happening. All morning she'd prepared herself to let go and now he was asking her to grab on. The difference was what she'd be holding on to.

Blayne stepped forward. "I had to tell him your plan. Give him a chance not to be an ass." She blew Ryker a kiss.

Then Claire joined her. "You got me bought into this plan. I wasn't about to let it all go to the wayside because the two of you were too stubborn to see you're made for each other. This is your second chance, Larkin. Don't pass it up. They don't always come." She grabbed Larkin's hand and squeezed. "By the way, you still owe me a bottle of moonshine."

Larkin bit her lip, sending a wary look toward Maxine's smiling face.

A breeze whispered through the trees and in the distance the melody of the Cape's wind chimes sang as familiar as Archer's laughter. A great rush of love and hope and happiness filled her chest and she threw herself into Ryker's arms.

"I never thought I'd love again or feel the lightness that comes with being happy. But with you I feel lighter, like anything is possible."

He buried his face in her neck. "No one understands that better than I do, cupcake. I figured I was too broken to be loved, but with you I feel like it just might be possible. You give me a peace I've never known before."

He gently fisted his hand in her hair and held her gaze. "I love you, Larkin. And that is the answer to everything."

Happiness bubbled through her chest. "I love you, too."

He froze at her words then without warning swept her up in his arms and captured her mouth in a hot, searing kiss full of moonlit promises and early morning secrets. Life with this man would never be dull.

"I've been dying without you. I can't wait to feel you, to taste you," he growled for her ears only.

Her heart skipped a beat as her body warmed to the idea immediately. She loved the heat of his touch, the sound of his voice, the way he hid a heart of gold behind his grumpy scowl. But even more, she loved being truly and deeply loved.

She'd been afraid to open up, afraid to move ahead as if it would be moving away from Archer, when all along, moving ahead honored her little boy's memory and kept him alive with every breath she took, every smile she gave, every day she lived.

She and Ryker could use their past to enrich their future.

She'd found an extraordinary *peace* in her puzzle.

Love fit perfectly...every time...on the Cape.

EPILOGUE

SIX MONTHS LATER

*L*arkin looked out over the crowd at Cape Van Buren Square with her heart so close to bursting she could barely breathe. It was time for the annual Fountain of Youth Festival, its amazing food and extraordinary live music marking the one hundred and thirty-eighth year since the healing waters had been discovered. She'd organized the event, and if her eyes didn't lie, the whole town had shown up.

Grateful was an understatement compared to what she was feeling, especially since it would be the last event she'd be in charge of for a while.

Ryker's warm hand slid under the open flap of her long puff coat and rubbed the steadily growing mound of her belly.

"How's our mini-cupcake?" His whisper in her ear sent a thrill down her spine. Would she ever get used to the rush of sensations and emotions the man evoked in her?

She sure as hell hoped not.

"I haven't thrown up for a whole fifteen minutes," she returned with a haughty raise of her brow.

He chuckled, his dark eyes dancing with a lightness that was new. "That's progress then."

Grabbing her hand, he brought her knuckles to his warm lips and pressed a kiss onto the platinum band on her ring finger. "Well, you already said I do, so there's no turning back now."

She held his gaze in challenge. "As if I could, and I'll never let you, so there you go."

"So there you go."

With a broad grin stretching his chiseled features wide, he kept her hand in his as they turned toward the excited crowd.

"I think you better welcome our guests before a riot breaks out," he chuckled.

Pulling in a deep breath, she checked the contents of her stomach on a brief pause and then shouted, "Ladies and gentlemen of Cape Van Buren, welcome to the one hundred and thirty-eighth annual Fountain of Youth Festival!"

Loud pops from both sides of the fountain could be heard over the commotion and sent clouds of confetti into the air.

The crowd's roar filled the town square at the sight. The Festival was as old as the town itself and as loved. Every February the citizens would brave blizzards and flurries for hot spiced apple cider, turkey thighs, and the North Cove Confectionery's cupcakes with frosting in the town's colors of turquoise and gold. Bands from all over the world would play for a chance to sip the legendary waters.

Larkin turned back to Ryker. "Thank you."

"For what?" He raised a dark brow in a way that reminded her of the day they met.

"For everything," she answered as her fingers searched beneath her scarf to the space on her chest where her locket rested but only met skin. "I hope Mrs. Peterson's able to get the locket back to me soon."

"What's going on, kids?" Maxine walked up with Claire and Blayne flanking her—as if the woman needed a posse. Larkin didn't even try to hide her grin as she kissed her sweet friend on the cheek and hugged the girls.

"Just kicking the party off. My mind wants a cupcake but I'm afraid my stomach's not listening," she said.

Blayne pointed at her rounding belly. "Auntie's going to have to have a word with that little munchkin if she doesn't ease up on the morning sickness already."

"She?" Ryker's cheeks paled and Maxine slipped an arm around her grandson's waist.

"She or he, you are going to make a fine father. I am so proud of you." She smiled up at him then glanced back to Larkin. "Speaking of fathers. Your mom and dad are grabbing cider and heading to the stage for the concert."

"Great. I'll go meet them. Getting off my feet sounds perfect right about now."

"Are you getting tired?" Claire's question was unexpected and very sweet.

"Yes, and the morning sickness isn't getting any better. I was barely able to finish my commitment to the festival with how bad I've been feeling. Speaking of commitments..." Larkin turned to Blayne. "I've initiated the not-for-profit paperwork for the community outreach, but I'm not going to be able to direct the project as I thought I was going to. I wanted to talk to you about it."

Blayne's eyes sparked with interest. "You know I'm your right hand, Lark."

"Now hold on just a second." Ryker interrupted. "I thought we talked about this?"

There was the scowling face she had come to love. It was all she could do to hide her grin. Sometimes, she said things just to see it once in a while. "We did. You have some old high school, college buddy you want to bring to town. I have a trusted friend already here."

She slipped her arm through Blayne's.

"I have to agree," Claire added.

"Me, too," Maxine chimed in, handing Claire a brown paper bag. "Here. I believe this is yours."

Claire wrapped her hand around the bagged bottle and squealed. She was finally getting her moonshine.

"Shhhhh!" Maxine admonished. "As much as I am for being the center of attention, this is not the time."

Ryker's eyes bounced between the women as he stepped forward. "Enough. It's all I can do not to drink that whole damn bottle right now being around you ladies." He turned to Larkin. "Jay knows how to handle things like this and with his family name, he can get it done faster."

Larkin sniffed. "Says you. Blayne's been in this town for years. Everyone knows her and loves her. She's been a part of this since the beginning. The town will work harder and faster for her than any out-of-towner you might bring in."

He raked a hand through his hair. "He's not an out-of-towner."

"But he lives out of town." She loved how his brows pulled tight as his frustration rose. It wasn't nice of her, but he was so damn sexy when he was all worked up.

"Cupcake, I swear—"

She planted a kiss on his mouth, effectively shutting down his argument. He immediately wrapped his arms around her and took the kiss deeper than she'd intended. It was becoming a habit. The man's passion was hard to keep up with but she looked forward to trying. She pressed into him as far as her growing belly would allow until the not too subtle clearing of a throat behind her grounded them back in reality.

Disentangling herself from the delectable man, she stepped back and peeked at Maxine's grinning face. Shit.

"Sorry."

"Well, I'm not," Ryker added. He put a hand out. "Before everyone runs off, I have something for Larkin, and I think it's something you might like to see."

That got everyone's attention, especially hers.

"You didn't have to do anything," she whispered. Between the Cape, him moving in with her, their very special wedding by the newly built well, the plans for the outreach program, and the new baby coming their way in a few months, she was about as happy as she could possibly stand.

Her hands rested on her tummy. Archer would have been an amazing big brother. Her throat tightened but she smiled.

He cleared his throat, suddenly looking nervous in a way she'd only seen once before. The night he'd proposed up in the lighthouse.

"What is it?"

He pulled the familiar purple velvet box from Peterson's Jewelry Box out of his pocket. "I hope this is okay. Since we were getting the chain fixed..." His gravelly words trailed off as she took the box with trembling hands.

Lifting the lid, she peered inside to find her locket. It sparkled a brilliant gold, buffed and polished by Cape Van Buren's world-class jewelers.

"Look at the back," Ryker said softly.

She took the necklace from the box, handing the case over to Blayne. Turning the locket over in her hand, her eyes blurred.

Engraved in the back read: *The answer to life's puzzle is love.*

Her fingers flew to her lips. "Oh, Ryker."

"There's more."

She glanced at him through tears in her eyes, then back at the locket and opened it.

Inside she found new photos. On one side was a baby picture with the title *Big Brother Archer* and on the opposite side a sonogram picture titled *Baby Van Buren*. Her chest tightened with so much emotion that she got a little light headed.

"Oh," she whispered. It was all she could manage around the lump in her throat.

"The sonogram's only temporary until we have an actual photo, but I wanted to help honor the special guardian angel our son or daughter will have. I still have your other photos, I'd never—"

Larkin stopped him with a kiss. "It's beautiful. It's more than everything," she whispered against his lips.

And it was.

She was no longer holding on to the last day she'd spent with Archer, but to the days she'd spend with his little brother or sister, to the memories of Archer's humor and wit and intelligence that she was sure to see in the little blessing heading their way. Archer was with her and around her as he'd always been and always would be.

Ryker pulled her into his side with a possessive grip as she showed the locket to her friends. Cape Van Buren was changing in meaningful and memorable ways.

And she was a part of it.

Now that she'd found love on the Cape, she had so much more to give.

Did you love *Love on the Cape*? Reviews make a huge difference to an author's career. I would be extremely grateful if you are able to take a few seconds and leave a review on your favorite retailer!

Don't forget to join my mailing list for your **FREE** copy of *Honor on the Cape*, and for new release alerts, a monthly self-exam reminder, and NO spam! Visit my website to sign-up!

ALSO AVAILABLE IN THE ON THE CAPE SERIES

Love on the Cape
Honor on the Cape
Cherish on the Cape
Draw You In
One Jingle or Two
Love, Honor & Cherish: The On the Cape Trilogy

ACKNOWLEDGMENTS

To my children and husband, otherwise known as my heart and soul, thank you for believing in me and always knowing I could do this even when I didn't. I love you. To my big brothers, Tommy, Todd, and Billy—as goofy as I am, you've always held me up. To Paula, my sister of the heart, I'm forever in awe of you. And to my mom, who's continued to mother me from the other side, I hope I have a fraction of your grace. Thank you.

Thank you to my editor KR Nadelson. It was such a pleasure having you on this journey with me. You really get me, and I loved getting to know you better. To my copy editor Jessica Snyder, you go above and beyond and are forever in my heart. Thank you to Dawn Yacovetta, KC Crocker, and Kristen Johnson for your eagle eyes while proofing this story! Errors are inevitable but with your help my readers will be distracted by a lot less.

Barbara O'Neal, thank you for your kind words about this story, and thank you for your guidance when I've had questions. Your friendship is cherished.

Thank you to Lucy Gage and Katana Collins for letting me chat with you about the beautiful state of Maine! You two are wicked smart! Lucy, your quick read and feedback were exactly what I needed. Thank you!

Sara Lunsford! You saved me with your generous heart. Thank you for formatting this book for me in my time of need.

Thank you, Kyung Min with SyMobius for my incredible Cape Van Buren logo! I absolutely love it.

Thank you to the Romantics, your love lifts me up, and to my street team, MK & CO, for your friendship and for believing in me. I love everyone in this family, from the very first to the still-to-come.

One more exuberant thank you to the readers of this book. Experiencing life with you in this way is magical. I hope that at least one scene, one line, or simply one word resonates with each of you. And to my sisters and brothers in the fight against breast and all types of cancer. I know both sides, having lost my mom to breast cancer at a young age, and having survived cancer myself. Now I'm facing a second time, but working on this book has given me something positive to focus on. By book two I'll be a survivor x 2! My writing is one of the things that carries me through. I have many more books to write.

Thank you. Hugs, loves, and peanut butter,
MK

ABOUT THE AUTHOR

 MK Meredith writes contemporary romance promising an emotional ride on heated sheets. She believes the best route to success is to never stop learning. Her lifelong love affair with peanut butter continues, and only two things come close in the battle for her affections: gorgeous heels and maybe Gerard Butler...or was it David Gandy? Who is she kidding? Her true loves are her husband and two children who have survived her SEAs (spontaneous explosions of affection) and lived to tell the tale. The Merediths live in the DC area with their large fur baby...until the next adventure calls.

www.mkmeredith.com

mk@mkmeredith.com

facebook.com/mkmkmeredith

twitter.com/mkmkmeredith

instagram.com/mkmkmeredith

bookbub.com/authors/mk-meredith

amazon.com/author/mk-meredith

ALSO BY MK MEREDITH

THE ON THE CAPE SERIES

Love on the Cape

Honor on the Cape

Cherish on the Cape

Draw You In

One Jingle or Two

Love, Honor & Cherish: The On the Cape Trilogy

THE SCRIPTED FOR LOVE SERIES

There's no place like paradise and the happy ever afters found in the film industry of Malibu, CA.

Love Under the Hot Lights

Just a Little Camera Shy

A Heated Touch of Action

THE INTERNATIONAL TEMPTATION SERIES

A strong dose of decadence along with a side of tall, dark, and sexy in your favorite travel destinations.

Playing the Spanish Billionaire

Seducing the Italian Tycoon

THE SEATTLE CRUSH SERIES

Seducing Seven

~